THE GUNSMITH

488

The Gunsmith Down Under

Books by J.R. Roberts
(Robert J. Randisi)

The Gunsmith series

Gunsmith Giant series

Lady Gunsmith series

Angel Eyes series

Tracker series

Mountain Jack Pike series

COMING SOON!
The Gunsmith
489 – Town Tamers

For more information
visit: www.SpeakingVolumes.us

THE GUNSMITH

488

The Gunsmith Down Under

J.R. Roberts

SPEAKING VOLUMES, LLC
NAPLES, FLORIDA
2024

The Gunsmith Down Under

ISBN 979-8-89022-137-7

Chapter One

San Francisco

Most of Clint Adams visits to San Francisco were spent in two gambling areas: Portsmouth Square and the Barbary Coast. The gambling houses of Portsmouth Square were very high class, catering to men and women who lived in wealthy neighborhoods like Nob Hill. Meanwhile, the Barbary Coast houses catered to a lower class clientele, such as sailors, docks workers, pickpockets and thieves.

Clint often stayed with friends when he was in town, but this time he had chosen a hotel he had never used before. It was just outside of Portsmouth Square, but it enabled Clint to easily walk there and gamble in such houses as The Parker House Saloon, Sam Dennison's Exchange and The El Dorado Gambling Saloon.

Gambling dens were also available in nearby China-town, but they were in among the many storefronts dealing in opium and other drugs. Clint had been to Chinatown, but not to imbibe any kind of drugs.

While most of Clint's time was spent gambling, he also made time for Portsmouth Square's female patrons. In a week, while he gambled and won, two women had come and gone, after some pleasant dalliances. He was just about to leave San Francisco when he ran into a surprise . . .

***

Clint was coming out of Samuel Dennison's Exchange after several successful hours of poker. He had enough money in his pocket to make the week in San Francisco well worth it.

If this was to be his last night in town he decided to have a good meal. The Crystal Palace had a first class steak house, so he headed that way. When he got there it was only half full. He was able to choose a table and place his order for a steak dinner. When the waiter brought the food Clint took his time eating, enjoying every bite. Once he collected his Tobiano from the livery and hit the trail, there was no telling when he would have another such meal. For at least a few nights on the trail, he would be eating bacon-and-beans.

"Anything else, Sir?" the waiter asked when he collected Clint's empty plate.

"What kind of pie do you have?"

"Several, Sir," the waiter said. "Apple, cherry, peach—"

"I'll take peach, and strong, black coffee."

"Coming up, Sir."

While waiting for his pie Clint took a look at the room. Most of the occupied tables held two or three people, mostly men, a few women. All were well-dressed, and may have just come from, or were heading for, a Portsmouth Square gambling house.

The few ladies who were present were in the company of men. That was fine with Clint, as he wasn't looking for company on his final night in town. He needed to get a good night's sleep for the miles ahead. He had no place in mind for his next stop, which meant he would probably just be riding aimlessly for a while. It was the kind of thing he liked to do after leaving a crowded city or town. He usually needed some time alone after being among people.

There was one woman he hadn't noticed when he first came in, probably because she was seated with her back to the door. Now, because of raised voices from that table, his attention was drawn there. It was the man who was speaking loudly in an annoyed tone.

"You ain't gettin' off that easy," the well-dressed man growled, loudly. The woman replied, saying something the man didn't like. "You think so?"

At that point the woman threw her napkin down on the table and stood up. The man also stood, quickly, knocking his chair over, and reached for her. She pulled away, but he reached again and grabbed her arm.

"You're not goin' anywhere without me," he snapped.

She swung her free arm and slapped him in the face. "You bitch!"

As he yanked her towards him, Clint sprang from his chair while other diners watched.

"That's enough!" he shouted.

The man looked at him and said, "This is none of your business, stranger."

"I'm making it my business," Clint replied. "Let go of her arm."

The man hesitated, then opened his hand, releasing the woman's arm.

"Do you know who I am?" he demanded.

"Right now you're just a man mistreating a woman," Clint said. "That's all I need to know."

"You're going to be sorry you stuck your nose in my business, friend," the man said.

"I think you better leave if you want to make that threat come true in the future," Clint said.

The man threw a murderous look at the woman, then stormed out.

When the woman turned towards Clint, the first thing he saw were her luminous blue eyes—blue eyes he had seen before.

"Meg?"

She smiled beautifully and said, "Hiya, mate."

Chapter Two

He hadn't seen Margaret "Meg" McGregor in three years. . .

***

. . . it was in a small town in Montana where they met. Clint was riding through and saw Meg on the street. Those blue eyes bore into him as he rode by, and later they met in a saloon she was running. She was a businesswoman who had owned establishments in several different towns, and had ended up owning a saloon in Wolfshead, Montana. But the denizens of Wolfshead were trying to force her out. Several men were sent into her place to break it up—tear it apart, actually—but they were unfortunate enough to try it while Clint was standing at the bar, drinking a beer. Clint used a few well-placed bullets to convince them to leave, and did it without killing any of them. Meg took him up to her room to show him her appreciation, and he didn't leave for three days. She convinced him that she would be able to take care of herself once he left . . .

***

He took her back to his table and bought her a piece of pie and some coffee, while he had a second cup and a slice of peach pie of his own.

"Who was that gent, Meg?" he asked.

"A former business partner," she told him.

"What was he so mad about?"

"He's not happy that I've decided to leave San Francisco, and I don't want to take him with me."

"Is he likely to cause trouble?"

"Oh, yes," she said, "but while I appreciate your help, I can handle him."

"That's what you told me about Wolfshead," he reminded her. "What happened after I left there?"

"Well, I hung on for a few more weeks, but eventually decided to move on. I've been in several towns since then, running different businesses."

"And now you're moving on from here," Clint said.

"Yes, but it's a bigger move," she said. "I'm going home."

"To Australia?" he asked.

"Yes, indeed. It seems I've been left a thriving business by a deceased relative."

"What kind of relative? Father?"

"No, no," she said. "My father died well before I left Australia, years ago. No, I'm not sure who the relative was, but the lawyer who wrote to me assures me that I have claim to the business, free and clear. I only have to go home and take control of it."

"What kind of business is it?"

"Apparently," she said, "it's a ranch."

"What do you know about ranching?"

"Not a thing," she said, "but there's supposed to be someone running it until I arrive."

"Meg," he said, "when were you last in Australia?"

"My, my," she said, "I left when I was sixteen, which is almost sixteen years ago."

"You sounded more Australian when I met you three years ago."

"I know," she said, "I've lost almost all of my accent."

"Are you sure you want to go back?" he asked.

"Why not?" she asked. "About the only nice thing to happen to me in the last sixteen years were the three days I spent with you in Wolfshead. You do remember those three days, don't you, mate?"

"Oh, I remember."

She smiled and asked, "How much longer will you be here in San Francisco?"

"I was intending to check out of my hotel tomorrow," he said.

"Then you still have a room for tonight?"

"I do."

"I don't suppose you have room for one more?" she asked. My ship leaves tomorrow and I need someplace to spend the night. We could relive those three nights before I leave the country."

"Do you have luggage?"

"I sent it on ahead to be loaded on the boat."

"Well then," he said, "I don't see any reason why I can't share my last night in my room."

"And share your bed?" she asked.

"Most definitely," he said, "but first finish your pie."

***

Clint remembered those three nights three years ago very well. And he remembered much more about Meg McGregor than just her blue eyes. She had the same long, auburn hair, and the same smooth skin and solid body, the same full, firm breasts and butt that he had spent those days exploring.

As soon as they entered his room, she turned and came into his arms, and they feverishly undressed each other.

"My God," she said, "I've missed you. I've missed this." She wrapped her hand around his hard cock.

As he moved to the bed with her, he realized he had also missed her. He often thought of those three days, and replayed them in his mind, but there was no longer any need for that. He had the real thing in his arms, once again.

Chapter Three

"You've missed me, too, haven't you?" she asked, as she lay in his arms later. "Admit it!"

"Oh, I admit it," he said. "I've thought about you a lot."

"And now we've had one more night together, and we'll go our separate ways again."

"That's right."

"Unless . . ."

He looked down at her and asked, "Unless what?"

She eased herself out of his arms and sat up, her bare breasts swaying slightly.

"I have a proposition for you."

"And what would that be?"

"Come with me."

"Come with—you mean, to Australia?"

"Why not?" she asked. "Where were you heading from here?"

"No place in particular."

"Have you ever been to Australia?"

"No."

"Ever been out of the country?"

"A time or two," he said. "England, South America."

"Lately?"

"No, not for a while."

"Then what's keeping you from coming with me?" she asked. "It'll be an adventure."

"I've had plenty of adventure in my life, as it is," Clint said.

"But this will be very different," Meg said. "Can ya imagine how we could spend the time on the boat? I have a cabin to myself."

"How long would we be on the boat?" he asked.

"I'm not even sure," she said, "but if we're together, who cares?" To make her point she slid her hand down between his legs to take hold of him. He began to get hard again. "I see you agree," she said, stroking him.

"Meg—"

"Think about it, Clint," she said, "while I do . . . this!"

She swooped down on him and took his cock into her mouth. As she sucked it, it became harder and harder. If she wanted him to think about her suggestion, she wasn't giving him much time to do it. All he could think about was her mouth.

As he felt an explosion rising up from inside him, she steadied herself with a hand on each of his thighs, and sucked him harder and faster, until he finally filled her mouth with his seed, accompanied by a mighty roar . . .

***

Some time later, when they had both regained their breath, she asked, "Well, what do you think?"

He had to admit, spending time with her in her cabin during the boat ride was an attractive proposition, but what would he do when they got there?

"Clint," she said, as if reading his mind, "I need your help. I'm not only asking you to come with me so we can fuck all the way there. When we arrive, I'm going to need someone to . . . well, be by my side while I figure out what I'm going to do."

One thing he liked about Meg back when he met her was that there was nothing silly about her. She was a mature woman then, and even moreso now.

What was keeping him from saying yes? She was right, it would be an adventure, the type he hadn't experienced since going to South America, years ago. And there was nothing coming up in the near future to keep him in America.

"Am I going to be able to get a ticket?" he asked. "I mean, if the boat's leaving tomorrow?"

"There'll be no problem, since you'll be staying in my cabin," she told him. "We can go to the docks after breakfast and make the arrangements." She propped herself up and looked into his eyes. "Will you come?"

"Why not?"

"Oh, yes!"

She grabbed him and kissed him hard, and then hugged him, pressing her bare breasts against his chest.

That led to more sex, and there would be plenty more to come . . .

***

In the morning they dressed and went down to the desk so Clint could check out. Then they left and headed for the train in a horse-drawn carriage.

"I don't have much in the way of luggage," he told her.

"That's no problem," she said. "I'll buy you a whole new wardrobe when we get there."

"I can buy my own clothes."

"Nonsense," she said. "When we get there I'm going to start paying you, and covering your expenses."

"Can you afford that?"

"When I was notified about my inheritance, the note was accompanied by money—a lot of money. So the answer is, yes, I can definitely afford it."

Chapter Four

The 4 day trip from San Francisco to New York by rail took its toll, and they were both exhausted when they reached Manhattan. Meg arranged for a hotel room for one night, and for once sex was out of the question. They both fell asleep and slept til morning.

When they reached the docks of New York, Clint was impressed with the sheer size of the ocean liner. He was still looking it over when Meg came back with his ticket.

"Come on, we can board," she said.

"This one?" he asked, pointing to the ship he had been admiring.

"That's the one, The Sea Princess."

They walked to the gangway and started up with other passengers, some of whom were carrying luggage, which they swung ahead of them to make their way. Clint and Meg stepped aside to let them pass, since they were all going to end up on the same ship.

"Like I told you before, I was smart enough to send my luggage ahead. With any luck, it's in my cabin."

"This is impressive," Clint said, as they reached the deck.

Meg moved ahead to speak to a purser, who directed her to her cabin.

"This way," she told Clint, leading the way.

Clint had decided not to have any second thoughts about his accompanying Meg to Australia. He was looking forward to nights of wild sex with her, but sex was not the main reason for his decision. He wanted to help Meg because he was very fond of her. But even that was not the main reason he was on the ship. In the end, it was the promise of an adventure unlike any he had seen in some time. And then there was the fact that no one in Australia would know who he was. Which meant there was no chance of anyone stepping up to try him, and even less chance of someone trying to shoot him in the back.

When they entered the cabin Meg was happy to see her luggage piled in the center of the floor.

"That's a lot of luggage," Clint commented, looking at the bags and chest.

"Well," she said, "after all, I'm moving sixteen years of life I've built up in America."

"I suppose that's true."

Clint could see the money Meg had spent on the room and furnishings, which were plush. It was a two-room suite with a large bed in the bedroom.

"This is pretty good," he said.

"It was the best I could get," she told him. "I wanted to be comfortable for the trip, and now that you're with me, I'm even happier with the accommodations." She turned and looked at him. "Why don't you relax while I unpack?"

"Unpack?"

"Well, not everything. Just a few things for the trip." Then she pointed to a sidebar against the wall. "I know, let's have a drink, first."

She went to the sidebar and asked, "Whiskey, or brandy?"

"I'll have whatever you have," he said, because what he really wished for was a beer.

She poured two glasses of brandy and walked to him with them.

"Here's to a wonderful trip, and a great adventure."

He accepted the glass, sat in a plush chair, and sipped while she unpacked a few things and put them in drawers.

The one thing about this trip that he was sorry about was that he had to leave his Tobiano in an unfamiliar livery stable for who knew how long? A trip to Australia was not going to be short. So, the day before, he had sent a telegram to his friend, John Locke, who had a ranch in Las Vegas, New Mexico. He asked if Locke could arrange to have Toby picked up and taken to his ranch, and kept there until he returned. He was sure his friend would do his best to care for the horse, so there was no worry there. With his mind at ease, he could enjoy the trip.

"How about we go and get something to eat?" he suggested.

"Oh, they won't be serving any food until we're underway," she assured him. "We have time."

He took her word for it and settled back into his chair. Clint Adams led the kind of life where there was very little time to relax. He always had to be ready for someone to make a try for him. But perhaps it would be different in the Sea Princess, and it should definitely be different once they arrived in Australia.

The trip would take nearly a hundred days, as they had to traverse both the Atlantic and Indian Oceans to reach Australia. Because the trip was that long, Meg felt she had to confess something to Clint.

"Confess what?" he asked, still seated in the chair.

"I really couldn't get you a ticket for this trip," she said.

"What?"

"There were none available, so I sort of . . . sneaked you in here,"

"You mean I'm a stowaway?"

"In essence, yes," she said. "I'm sorry, but I really needed you to come with me."

He stared at her for a few moments, and then had to laugh.

"Now I can see what you meant by this trip being an adventure."

"So you're not mad?"

"Oh," he said, "you bet I'm mad, but what can I do about it now?"

"I'll bring you your meals from the dining room, but you won't be able to leave this cabin."

"Oh, I'll leave," he said. "I'll take walks late at night. I'm not staying cooped up for a hundred or more days."

"Even with me?"

He laughed again and said, "Even with you."

Chapter Five

Sydney, Australia

Alan Carstairs looked up from his desk as his office door opened and Edward Hopkins entered.

"What have you got for me?" he asked.

"She's on her way."

"You're sure?"

"Yes, Sir."

"When will she arrive?"

"Roughly . . . three months."

Carstairs made a face.

"I hate waiting that long.

"She's the only one, Mr. Carstairs."

"Yes, yes, all right," Carstairs said. "Well, at least that gives us time to get everything ready."

"Yes, Sir."

"And you've found someone who had no qualms about killing a woman?"

"Yes, Sir, I have," Hopkins said. "There won't be a problem."

"Now, remember, I don't want her killed as soon as she gets off the boat. We have to get her to the Outback to look at the property, and then convince her to sell it to me."

"Yes, Sir."

"And if she won't sell it, then we kill her."

"Yes, Sir."

" 'Yessir, yessir,' I don't just want a yes man, Edward, I want to know that you're with me on this."

"I'm with you, Alan," Hopkins said, "All the way."

"I don't like having a woman killed, but I believe once she sees the property, it will be the only way."

"Then why show it to her in the first place?" Hopkins asked. "Why send her money to come home?"

"Because everything has to be done legally, Ed," Carstairs said. "We're civilized now."

"The Aborigines ain't."

"Well, we are," Carstairs said. "And we do things by the book."

"Except for murder," Hopkins said.

"Only when it's necessary," Carstairs said. "Remember that."

"I will Alan."

"You know," Carstairs said, "I think I liked it better when you were calling me 'sir.'"

"Yes, Sir."

"Now get out," Carstairs said, "and make sure everything is going according to plan."

"How do I do that?"

"Get out there," Carstairs said.

"The Outback?"

"That's right, the Outback," Carstairs said. "Make sure everybody knows what to do."

"Uh, sir, we have three months."

"About three months," Carstairs said. "I don't want any surprises." He stood up from his desk. "I'll be home. Don't disturb me unless it's an emergency."

"Yes, Sir."

"Oh, wait."

Hopkins turned.

"Do we have someone on the boat with her?"

"We do."

"A reliable man?"

"Reliable, and efficient."

"But he's been told what to do, right?" Carstairs asked.

"Yes," Hopkins said, "he's just going to watch her."

"All right, then," Carstairs said, "that's all."

Hopkins turned and left. Carstairs gave him time to get out of the building before he also left.

***

When Carstairs entered his home he called out, "Are you here? You better be here."

The girl came out of the bedroom and said, "I-I'm here."

"What are you wearing?" Carstairs demanded.

"Um, it's a nightgown, Mr. Carstairs."

"How many times have I told you, when I come home I want you *naked.*"

"Yes, Sir," she said, "but I didn't know you would be so early."

"Well then, get naked now and wait for me in there."

"Y-yes, Sir."

She started to peel the nightgown off as she turned to go back into the bedroom.

"No, wait," he said.

She turned and said, "Sir?"

"Wait until I come in to take it off," he said. "Wait on the bed."

"Yes, Sir."

"And don't forget, you're lucky to be here and not in the Outback with the rest of your people."

"Yes, Sir."

She went into the bedroom.

Carstairs went to the bar and poured himself a stiff drink. His business was going well, and he was enjoying this girl he had taken from the Outback, in his private life.

But the thing that was bothering him was having to deal with the McGregor girl for that Outback station. If she found out what was in that ground, she would never sell it to him, or anyone else. Then he would have no choice but to have her killed. But he wouldn't know which he was doing for three months.

When he was this stressed, there was only one way to work it off. He drained his drink, put the glass down, and went into the bedroom.

The girl was on the bed, waiting.

"Okay, darlin'," Carstairs said, "stand up and take it off, but do it slowly."

The girl stood. She was an Aborigine, dark-haired, dark skinned. As she peeled the nightgown from her frame, her long, lean body came into view, with brown nipples and a dark pubic patch.

"That's my girl," Carstairs said, "now come on over here and undress me, and we'll get to fucking . . ."

Chapter Six

Clint spent the first three days in the cabin, with Meg bringing him his meals. Then, at night, they spent their time in bed. But after three days he felt he needed to take a walk on deck.

"Are you sure, Clint?" Meg asked, from the bed. "You're gonna leave this warm bed, with me in it?"

"I'll be back, Meg," Clint said. "I just need to stretch my legs."

"Well, if somebody asks . . ."

"Don't worry," he said, "I won't give anyone a reason to ask questions."

"I'll be waiting right here," she told him, pulling the sheet away to reveal her nudity, "just like this."

He stared at her full breasts with their coral colored nipples, and then forced himself to go out the door.

It was after midnight, so there wasn't anyone else walking the deck. He passed many other cabins with the lights out, where other passengers were sleeping. He stayed away from parts of the ship where sailors were doing their jobs. He stopped to lean on the rail and look out at the water. He became aware of someone approaching him. He turned his head and watched the man carefully. He was tall, in good shape, and didn't seem to have a gun on him.

"Good evenin', mate," the man said. "Looks like I'm not the only one who needed some night air."

"I'd rather walk now than during the day, when there are people around," Clint said.

"I don't blame ya," the man said. "My name's Ben Wheeler."

"Clint. You're obviously Australian," Clint said. "Going home?"

"Yes, indeed," Wheeler said. "Been away a couple of years. That's long enough. I'm looking forward to getting back to the Outback."

"The Outback?"

"It's our version of your Mohave Desert."

"With Indians?"

"No," Wheeler said, "we call 'em Aborigines."

"Any animals out there?"

"Plenty," Wheeler said. "Cockatoos, kangaroos, koalas, alligators, dingos—"

"Dingos?" Clint asked. "What's a dingo?"

"A dog," Wheeler said, "but they're feral."

"Sounds like a wild place."

"It used to be wilder," Wheeler said. "Now there are ranches popping up all over, as we try to get along with the Aborigines, and animals."

"You have a ranch there?"

"My family does," Wheeler said. "When I get back I'll be taking over running it. You goin' there on business or pleasure?"

"A little bit of both."

"Well," Wheeler said, "maybe we'll run into each other there."

"Probably not in the Outback," Clint said.

"Maybe in Sydney, then, when we dock," Wheeler said. "Enjoy the rest of the trip. We'll probably see each other again. It's a long way."

"So I understand."

"Well," Wheeler said, " 'night."

" 'night," Clint said.

The man walked on. Clint watched him until he was out of sight around a corner. The man didn't seem concerned that Clint was wearing a gun on the ship. Clint figured he wouldn't need it, but he still wasn't comfortable enough to walk around without it. Maybe once they arrived in Sydney he would be comfortable enough to give it a try. It had been a long time since he walked around in public without a gun.

Chapter Seven

As Clint re-entered the cabin, Meg stood in the doorway to the bedroom, wearing only a filmy night-gown.

"I knew you'd be back soon," she said.

"I met a man on deck," Clint said. "An Australian. Taught me some things about the Outback."

"What man?" she asked, looking concerned. "What was his name?"

"Wheeler," Clint said, "Ben Wheeler. Do you know him?"

"Not him," she said, "but the Wheeler family has a ranch in the Outback."

"The Outback doesn't sound like a place I'd want to go," Clint said. "Alligators? Dingos?"

"They won't bother you if you don't bother them."

She walked across the room and poured two brandies, handed one to Clint.

"What are you trying to tell me?" he asked. "Are we going to the Outback?"

"I didn't want to tell you anything until we got to Sydney," she said.

Clint sat in a chair and crossed his legs.

"Okay, let's hear it."

"I'm supposed to meet with a lawyer in Sydney, to sign some papers."

"And then?"

"And then I'd be the owner of a station in the Outback," she said.

"So we have to go there to look the property over?" Clint asked.

"That's right," she said.

"What do you want to do with it? Sell it?"

She shook her head.

"It's been in my family a long time. One of the first."

"Aren't you worried about Aborigines?"

"No," she said, "over the years my family has formed a good relationship with them. My aunt and uncle kept them fed and clothed."

"Aunt and uncle?" Clint asked. "No father, or mother?"

She shook her head.

"No, my parents have been dead a long time. My Aunt died a few years ago. Now my uncle has died, and left the property to me."

"I see."

"Now you know why I wanted you to come with me," she said. "I need to be with someone I can trust."

"We spent three days together three years ago," he said.

"That was long enough," she said. "I trust you."

"So you and the Wheelers own ranches in the Outback," Clint said, "and now you and Ben Wheeler are on the same ship. Is that a coincidence?"

"It must be," she said. "There's no other way to get there. I'll bet a few more neighbors are aboard."

She finished her drink and put the glass down.

"Let's go to bed," she said. "We have a lot more nights ahead of us to talk."

He stood, set down his glass and put his arms around her.

"Who wants to talk?" he asked.

***

After several weeks, Meg had told Clint a lot about Sydney, and the Outback. Apparently some towns had also been built there. Some of them could be reached by train, and some on horseback.

He hadn't seen Ben Wheeler again, but when he went out for his midnight walks, he felt someone was watching him. He didn't think he would be taking his gun off once they reached Sydney.

He was sitting in a chair when Meg came out of the bedroom, dressed for the day.

"I'll bring back your breakfast," she promised.

"Have yours first," he said.

"No," she said, "I'll bring back enough for both of us."

"Be careful," he said, as she went to the door.

"About what?"

"Like you said a while back," Clint said. "Neighbors."

"Ben Wheeler? Have you seen him again?"

"Not for weeks," Clint said. "But I still feel like I'm being watched."

"By him?"

"Could be. I've been thinking about it. He suggested we'd probably see each other again, but we haven't."

"Then maybe he's taking his walks in the daytime."

"Keep an eye out for him," Clint said. "A tall man in good shape, maybe forty."

"I'll stay alert," she promised. "Ham-and-eggs?"

"That's fine," Clint said. "But when we get to Sydney they'll have steak, right?"

"Oh yes," she said, laughing. "The best. Wagyu steaks."

"Wagyu?"

"It's Japanese, but they crossbreed with cattle from other countries, including Australia. You'll see. When we get there, you'll enjoy it."

She rushed out the door to fetch breakfast.

Chapter Eight

When she returned, they talked over breakfast of ham-and-eggs, biscuits and coffee.

"Any sign of Wheeler?" he asked.

"No one seemed to be paying special attention to me," she said.

"A woman as beautiful as you?" he asked. "That can't be true."

"Well, yes," she said, "that kind of attention. But not the kind you seem to be worried about."

"That's good," he said.

"So what are you going to do today?" she asked.

"What? I'm going to try something," he said.

"A walk around the deck."

"In the daylight?"

"Yes."

"You know if they find out you're a stowaway they'll toss you in the brig," she warned.

"And why would anyone believe I'm a stowaway after almost a month at sea," he asked. "We haven't made any stops."

"I think I should walk with you," she said. "Maybe that way no one will even ask."

She stood, linked her arm in his, and they went out the door.

***

As they made a circuit of the deck Clint became aware that there was a lower and higher deck. And the bridge, where the Captain was.

"No one is paying special attention to us," Meg said.

"Not obviously," Clint said, "but we're still being watched."

"But why?"

"There can only be two reasons," he said. "You or me."

"Why would anyone be watching me?" she asked.

"That's a good question," Clint said. "If someone *is* watching you, then there's more to this inheritance than meets the eye, and it was probably a good idea to bring me along."

"I thought it was," she reminded him.

"But if someone is watching me, there is probably the obvious reason."

"Because of who you are?" she asked.

"Exactly."

"But we've been on board for almost a month," she said, "and no one has tried to kill you. Or put you into custody as a stowaway."

They nodded a greeting to other passengers they passed. Suddenly, a uniformed young man appeared in front of them.

"Miss MacGregor," he said. "I am the ship's purser. My name is Louis. I have a message for you from the Captain."

"What would that message be?" she asked.

"He would like you to dine with him at the Captain's Table tonight," Louis said, then looked at Clint. "You and your . . . companion."

Before Meg could speak, Clint said, "We'd be happy to join the Captain."

"Excellent," Louis said, "seven p.m. please."

"We'll be there," Meg said.

"I'll inform the captain." Louis walked away.

"What do you suppose that's about?" Meg asked.

"I guess we're going to find out at dinner," Clint said. "I'll just be happy to eat at a regular table, rather than in our cabin."

"What if the captain asks to see your ticket?" Meg asked.

"I guess we'll deal with that when the time comes," Clint said.

"Clint," she said, "I'm going to be very upset if you get put in the brig as a stowaway."

"I think I'll be pretty upset about that, as well," he said, and steered her back to their cabin.

***

Meg wore a beautiful dress for their dinner at the Captain's Table, showing off her bare shoulders and the upper slopes of her breasts. Clint had to simply wear the best clothes he had, after getting them as clean as he could. He also wore his gun.

When they entered the dining room on the upper deck, Louis greeted them at the door.

"The Captain's Table is this way," he told them. "He's waiting for you. Follow me, please."

He led them across the room to a table where a man in his fifties was waiting, wearing a white captain's uniform. As they approached he stood and smiled.

"Miss McGregor?" he asked.

"That's right."

"I'm Captain Farmington," he said. "Thank you for agreeing to dine with me. You look lovely."

"Thank you."

"And your companion?"

Clint and Meg had already agreed that she would simply introduce him, and they would see what happened.

"This is Clint Adams."

Farmington looked surprised.

"Well," he said, "I was unaware that we had such an esteemed man on board." He gave his purser a hard look.

"Oh, uh, I didn't know either, Sir."

"That'll be all, Louis," the Captain said. "Please, Miss McGregor, Mr. Adams, sit. I'm hoping you'll enjoy dinner."

Chapter Nine

It was obvious to Clint that the purser was responsible for letting the captain know who was on board, especially if it was someone well known.

The reason for the invitation to dine with the captain was not readily identifiable. It was only the three of them at the table that had room for eight.

As soon as they were seated, waiters began to appear carrying trays covered with plates of food.

"I had our chef prepare several different dishes, so that you would have a choice."

As the trays were set on the table in front of them, Clint left it to Meg to choose.

"That's the Wagyu beef I was telling you about," she said, pointing. "Apparently we won't have to wait to arrive in Sydney to enjoy it."

"Suits me," Clint said, using his fork to spear a large slab. After that he used serving spoons to surround the meat with several different vegetables.

"I can offer you whiskey," the Captain said, "wine or beer."

"I'll take wine," Meg said.

"White or red?"

"Red."

"And you, Mr. Adams?"

"Beer, please."

"Of course."

They soon had everything in front of them that they would need and began eating.

"No doubt you're wondering why I invited you to dine with me," the Captain said.

Clint left it to Meg to answer.

"The thought had crossed my mind," she said.

"When I was told there was an extraordinarily beautiful woman on board, I naturally wanted to meet her. And when I was told she was accompanied by the Gunsmith—well, I just had to invite you both to dinner."

Clint and Meg exchanged a glance.

"So you knew I was on board," Clint said.

"Oh yes, almost immediately."

"Then why wait this long to make contact?" Clint asked.

"Well, to tell you the truth, up until now there was no reason to make contact," Captain Farmington said. "Of course I would have still enjoyed the company of Miss McGregor, but something else has come up."

"And what's that?"

"It's come to my attention that there are some men on board who intend to take over the ship."

"When?"

"As we approach Sydney," Farmington said. "So, roughly in two months' time."

"And you want help handling them?"

"I want them identified," Farmington said, "and then dealt with."

"Dealt with?"

"Must I spell it out, Mr. Adams?" Farmington asked. "I want them killed."

"And what makes you think I would do that?"

"Well, Sir, for one thing, I know your reputation as a legendary gunfighter. And on the other hand, I doubt you would want to spend the rest of this trip in the brig as a stowaway."

"And what makes you think I'm a stowaway?"

"Mr. Adams," Farmington said, "if I were to ask to see your ticket right now, what would you do?"

"I would go down to my cabin and get it."

"Your cabin?" the Captain asked. "I don't have any record of you having a cabin. I think you mean Miss McGregor's cabin. But let me save you the time. You don't have a ticket."

Clint cut a large chunk of meat and put it into his mouth, just in case it was to be his last bite of food.

"But relax, Sir," the Captain said. "I don't have any intention of placing you in the brig. After all, what help would you be to me, there?"

"Don't you have your own security force?" Clint asked.

"My crew are not trained in military matters," Farmington said.

"So how many men are we talking about?" Clint asked.

"I'm not sure."

"How many could take over the ship?" Clint asked.

"If they're well-trained and well-placed, perhaps a dozen or so. They would need to take over the bridge, communications center, and engine room."

"And you expect me to kill a dozen or so men?"

"Not alone, of course," Farmington said. "Since the takeover won't happen until we're almost in Sidney, you have plenty of time to train my men to back you up."

"I see," Clint said. "You want me to train your men to repel this takeover."

"Exactly."

"Well," Clint said, "since I have time to train your men, I also have time to give this some thought." He looked at Meg. "Would you like some champagne?"

"I Would love some."

Chapter Ten

After they finished their dinner, a bottle of champagne, coffee and pie. The Captain ordered after-dinner drinks.

"Well, Mr. Adams," Captain Farmington said, when they had their glasses of brandy, "What have you decided?"

"Oh," Clint said, "you want me to decide this right here and now? I thought I'd have a day or two to think about it."

"There's not much of a decision to make," the Captain said. "You either decide to help me, or spend the rest of this trip in the brig. It's that simple."

"Wow, you're not giving me much of a choice," Clint said. "And one more thing."

"What is that?"

"We're talking about piracy."

"Correct."

"And that's the reason you want them all dead."

"Yes," Farmington said, "It's what pirates deserve."

"So I suppose the answer is yes."

"Excellent!" the Captain said. "Very good. Tomorrow you'll be meeting the men you will be training to back you up."

"And I suppose I have the run of the ship?"

"Definitely," the Captain said. "You may go anywhere you like, at any time."

"Well, that'll be better than staying in Meg's cabin all day and sneaking out at night."

The Captain pushed back his chair and said, "Now I must take my leave. You may stay at my table as long as you want." He bowed to Meg and said, "Madam, it was a delight to meet you. Mr. Adams, I'm at your disposal day or night. Just let Louis know."

"Thank you," Clint said, standing.

As the captain left, Clint sat back down and scooted his chair closer to Meg's.

"Well," he said, "I thought we were going to be on the lookout for Mr. Wheeler, but it turns out to be the Captain."

"Are you gonna do it?" she asked.

"You heard the man," Clint said. "I either train his men, or spend the rest of the trip in the brig. That's not much of a choice."

"But he wants you to kill those men before they can take the ship over."

"That's not going to happen," Clint said. "I'll train his men to handle whatever comes along."

"Do you think you can?"

"I won't know the answer to that until I see what I'm working with."

"And that will happen tomorrow."

"Yes."

"Clint," she said, "I'm starting to feel sorry I made you come on the ship with me."

"You and I have things to take care of in Australia, Meg," Clint said. "Let's go back to the cabin."

***

As they entered, Clint stopped short.

"What is it?" she asked, in a whisper.

"No need to whisper," he said. "No one's here now, but I think someone was."

"But why?"

"To take a look around."

"For what?"

"Who knows?"

"Should we look around?" she asked.

"You get changed," he said. "Get comfortable, and I'll take a look."

"All right."

She went into the bedroom and closed the door. Clint inspected the room, although he didn't know what he was looking for. He was sitting in a chair when she opened the door and came out of the bedroom, wearing a nightgown.

"Anything?" she asked.

"No," Clint said, "if someone was in here, they were very good."

"One of the crew?"

"I doubt it. Somebody who knew what they were doing. Nothing is out of place."

"What if they weren't looking for anything," she suggested, "but planting something."

"I thought about that," Clint said. "I didn't see anything."

"Should we move to another cabin?"

"No," Clint said, "then we'd have to go through the whole thing all over again."

"Well," she said, "I suppose we'd better go to bed."

"I want to sit up a while," he said. "But when I go to bed I'll want to get some sleep. I assume someone will be knocking on our door very early."

"We'll see about that," she said, and went into the bedroom.

She was either commenting on whether or not someone would be knocking on their door early, or the fact
that he said, he would be going to sleep.

Chapter Eleven

As he predicted, there was a knocking on the cabin door early the next morning. Clint was dressed, so he closed the bedroom door before answering. The purser, Louis, stood there.

"Good morning, Mr. Adams."

"Louis."

"I've got your men waiting in the main salon for you."

"What about breakfast?"

"Also in the main salon."

"And other passengers?"

"The salon's closed to them."

"Okay," Clint said. "I'll be right there."

"I'll keep the coffee hot," Louis said.

"Thanks."

"How about the lady?"

"She'll be fine."

Louis nodded and started off along the deck.

As Clint closed the door, Meg opened the bedroom door and stepped out.

"I suppose you're going to be busy this morning."

"I suppose so," Clint said. "Why don't you stay inside."

"Sure," she said. "It's your turn to bring me some breakfast."

"I won't be long," he said. "I just want to meet these men, get a good look at them."

"I'll get dressed while you're gone," she said. "That is, unless you don't want me to."

"You better get dressed, in case somebody comes to the door."

He strapped on his gunbelt and put on his hat.

"I'll be back soon."

He left and made his way to the main salon on the third deck. As he walked in he could smell bacon and coffee. Six men looked up from their plates as he entered. Three more were standing at a table, filling their plates. One of them was Louis. Except for the purser, they were all dressed like sailors.

"Breakfast is served," the purser said. "Help yourself and I'll make the introductions."

"I don't need to know everybody's name," Clint said. "As long as they do what they're told."

"They'll do whatever you tell 'em to do" Louis said. "Those are the Captain's orders."

Clint filled a plate with eggs and bacon, and poured himself a cup of coffee.

"All right," he told Louis. "Sit over here with me."

They walked to an isolated table, away from the others and started to eat.

"What have I got here, Louis?" Clint asked,

"These are the men who've been with the Captain the longest. They pretty much consider this ship theirs."

Clint looked over at the men, saw that most were of an age, forty or fifty.

"What about you?" Clint asked. "You're a lot younger than they are."

"I'm just markin' time until something better comes along," Louis said.

"Do they have guns?"

"We have an armory, of sorts," Louis said.

"I'll want to see it later today."

"No problem."

"What are their jobs?"

"A couple of 'em work on the bridge, a few others in the boiler room, others are deckhands."

"Can they fight?"

"As well as any man, I guess," Louis said. "They ain't soldiers."

"I'm starting to think I may be in trouble."

"They'll pull their weight," Louis said. "This tug is their home, they're not going to wanna give it up to a bunch of pirates,"

"Does the Captain figure the pirates are already aboard?"

"We heard a story before we pulled out of New York," Louis said. "There'll be a few of them already on board, but others will come up on us and threaten to blow us out of the water if we don't stop."

"Cannons?"

"I don't know what else they'd use."

"If they've got cannons there's not much we could do about it."

"I guess the Captain's hopin' you'll think of something."

"I'd count on me on solid ground," Clint said. "I don't know anything about fighting pirates."

"The Captain's got experience," Louis said. "Talk to him about it."

"Why's he need me, then?"

"He heard your name before we left," Louis said. "Somebody recognized you."

"And he waited this long?"

"You better sit down and talk," Louis said, "just you and him."

"What's that going to get us?" Clint asked.

"I figure between the two of you, you'll figure something out."

Chapter Twelve

When all had finished breakfast, except for some extra coffee, Clint stood in the center of the room.

"My name is Clint Adams," he said. "The Captain has asked me to speak with you on a matter that pertains to all of us—piracy."

A man raised his hand and stood.

"Some of us know your name, and some even recognize you, but what do you know about pirates?"

"Nothing," Clint said, "but I know about fighting."

"We know about fighting," another man said, as the first man sat down.

"You know about brawling," Clint countered. "What do you know about fighting to kill?"

The men looked around at each other.

"Why do we have to kill?" one asked.

"How else do you think you'd stop a band of pirates from taking the ship?" Clint asked. "If you're not willing to kill to save the ship, get up and walk out now."

Again, they looked around at each other. One or two seemed to want to stand and leave, but in the end they all stayed.

"All right, then," Clint said. "Let's see what we're dealing with."

***

Before telling the group of men what he wanted them to do, Clint had to discover what they could do. In the end he found three or four men who had once been in a war. He broke them into two groups of six, with each group having two experienced men. Then he broke them into two shifts, with one shift on duty, and one shift ever ready. Then he let eight men go and spoke to the other four—and Louis—in more detail about what he expected from them.

"What about the armory?" Clint asked Louis. "Who's in charge of that."

Louis pointed and said, "Silas, here. We don't have a lot of weapons, but he's the armorer."

"Okay, Silas," Clint said, "you and I are going to go down to the armory and have a look."

"All right with me," Silas said. He was a big, beefy man with short, salt-and-pepper hair, a thick neck and hands. Clint decided he would be good at hand-to-hand.

"What do the rest of us do?" a man asked.

"Nothing, for now. I just wanted to meet all of you. We'll go into more detail later." He stood and said, "Silas, take me to the armory."

"I'll come along, too, if you don't mind," Louis said.

"Suit yourself," Clint said. "The rest of you can go back to your regular duties."

Three of the men stood and left the salon. The fourth stood and turned to Clint.

"If you don't mind, I'll come to the armory with you. I know somethin' about guns."

"What's your name?"

"Rory Ames."

"Okay, Rory, come along." Clint looked at Louis. "Which way?"

"The deck below this one," Louis said.

While Louis and Silas led the way, Clint and Rory trailed along behind.

"If you know about guns," Clint said, "why aren't you the armorer?"

"I don't get along with the Captain, so he's got me swabbing the decks."

"How do you know about guns?"

"I grew up with 'em," Rory said. "If I hadn't taken to the sea as a young man, I probably would've gotten killed tryin' to be a gunman."

"What's your weapon of choice?"

"A rifle," Rory said. "I can pretty much hit whatever I aim at."

"We're going to see about that," Clint assured him.

***

Silas took out a key and unlocked the metal door. As Clint entered, he saw that it was a poor excuse for an armory.

He turned and looked at the other men.

"Do any of the men have their own guns?"

"The Captain don't allow it," Louis said. "He once had a mutiny on board. He don't want that to happen again."

"Well," Clint said, "it looks like he might be facing worse."

Clint turned to look at the arrangement of rifles and pistols hanging on the wall and piled in corners. He picked through them, then turned and looked at Silas.

"This is the way you care for your arms?" he asked.

"Hey," Silas said, "the Captain made me the armorer. I didn't say I wanted the job."

"Well then, you don't have it anymore," Clint said.

"Suits me," Silas said.

"Rory, you're the armorer now."

"How do you know I'm any better than Silas, here? the man asked.

"We're going to find out."

Chapter Thirteen

Clint put Rory and Silas to work, picking out the best of the rifles and pistols then getting them oiled and ready to fire.

"When you're done with that," Clint said, "collect all the ammunition and get ready to take these weapons out on deck. We're going to see how they fire."

"And what're you gonna do in the meantime?" Rory asked.

"Louis is taking me up to the Captain," Clint said. "I've got some things to discuss with him."

They left the two men in the armory and Louis took Clint to the bridge.

"Good morning, Mr. Adams," Captain Farmington said. "Have you seen your men?"

"I've seen them," Clint said.

"Are you going to be able to make a cohesive group out of them?"

"That's something we'll have to see," Clint said. "Right now we're working on the armory."

"It's not much, I know," Farmington said, "but it's what we have."

"I heard you've dealt with mutiny before," Clint said. "Why wouldn't you have a fully functional armory after that?"

"It's because I once had a fully equipped armory used in a mutiny against me. I vowed it would never happen again."

"That's fine for a mutiny," Clint said, "what about piracy?"

The Captain looked chagrined.

"To tell you the truth, I thought piracy was a thing of the past," he admitted. "You know, the Jolly Roger and all that crap."

"How many on your crew do you trust?"

"These days the crew isn't as much of a family as it used to be," the Captain said. "I gave you the men I thought I could trust."

"And how many of your men are you dead sure are not pirates, themselves?" Clint asked.

"I was hoping you'd weed them out for me," the Captain admitted.

"How am I supposed to know who's a pirate and who isn't?" Clint asked.

"I thought you'd be a better judge of men we could trust," Farmington said.

"You're putting a lot on my head, Captain," Clint said.

"Mr. Adams," the Captain said, "you're all I've got. In the future I intend to put together a more reliable crew."

"That is," Clint said, "if your ship even has a future."

"I have no intention of this being the Princess' last trip," the Captain said.

"I have the same intention," Clint said. "I was planning on taking your ship back home."

"Then we're on the same page," the Captain said.

"As far as what we're planning and hoping, yes," Clint said. "It remains to be seen what happens."

"What else can I do for you?" the Captain asked.

"Your armory offers slim pickings, to be honest," Clint said. "Some of those weapons are rusted, and won't even fire. Do you have any others hidden away?"

"I have a small stash I intended to only use in case of another mutiny."

Clint wondered how much better these hidden away weapons would be?

"Well, I think we're going to have to bring them out," Clint said.

The Captain thought a moment, then took a key from his pocket.

"Louis can take you to them," he said.

Clint turned and handed the key to Louis.

"Let's go."

***

Louis led Clint to another door on the third deck.

"The Captain's quarters is down there," Louis said, inclining his head. "I guess we can call this the Captain's armory."

He fitted the key into the lock and turned it. As he opened the door Clint saw a room smaller than the main armory, but better equipped. He could even smell gun oil, which meant the weapons were probably well cared for. What he saw was mostly Springfield and Winchester rifles, and a few handguns, including a few that looked European.

Clint put his hands on those and said, "These automatics look German. In the right hands, they'll be formidable."

"Yeah, but whose hands?" Louis asked. "Other than yours, of course."

Clint put his hand on his holstered Peacemaker and said, "I'll stick to my own gun. We're going to have to figure out whose hands to put these into."

"When?"

"No time like the present," Clint said. "Let's get all the men together on deck for some shooting."

Chapter Fourteen

Clint found all the men gathered on deck. There was a collection of passengers watching to see what was going on. Clint decided not to chase them away. Let them imagine it was some sort of entertainment.

There was a collection of weapons against the wall. They had been oiled and taken from the main armory. Clint brought four German automatics from the Captain's armory, along with a few Winchesters and Springfields.

He had each man fire a rifle and an automatic, tried to figure out who was most comfortable with what, and then had them go again, firing out to sea. It was difficult to figure out who was the most accurate without targets.

Clint decided to send two men down to the galley.

"They must have some old plates down there we could use as targets," he said, as the two men left.

"Where do you want to set them up?" Louis asked.

Clint thought a moment, then said, "I have an idea."

When the men returned Clint was surprised at how many plates each carried.

"The cook says he's been planning on getting rid of these," one of the men said.

"Okay, set them over there by the rail, and stand by them."

The men did that.

"Okay," he said, addressing the men, "we're going to toss plates out in the ocean and fire at them. Like this." He looked at the two men. "One at a time toss a plate as high and as far as you can."

"When?" one man asked.

"When I say 'throw.' Ready? Throw!"

Each man, in turn, flung a plate out as far and as high as he could. When it reached the apex of its arc, Clint drew and fired, twice, shattering each plate as it reached its highest point.

"Got it?" he told the man.

"You gotta be kiddin'," one of the men said.

They tried it twenty-four times, twice for each man. Only two of them managed to shatter a plate.

"Okay, we're wasting plates," Clint said. "Let's see if first we can learn how to shoot before we start firing at targets."

He worked for the next hour with each man individually. Rory and Silas were the two who managed to shatter one plate each. At one point Clint noticed that Meg had joined the crowd that was watching.

Clint found the eight men he wanted to arm with rifles, and the four—including Rory and Silas—to arm with automatics.

"Hey," Louis said, "how about me?"

Clint looked at the young purser.

"Do you have any experience shooting a gun?"

"No."

"Any experience at hand-to-hand combat?"

"No."

"We'll just keep you as liaison between me and the Captain then," Clint said. "In fact, supervise the tossing of the plates as we try that again."

As the men took turns tossing plates so that they could all fire, Clint walked over to Meg and pulled her aside.

"I thought I told you to stay in the cabin."

"I heard shooting, and wanted to see what's going on. You're very good with a gun. I saw you shatter those plates."

"Yes, I am," Clint said. "That's more than I can say for these sailors."

"You'll whip them into shape," Meg said.

"I hope you're right."

"Do you really think we're going to have to deal with pirates?" she asked.

"That's what the Captain thinks," Clint said. "After seeing what I have to work with, I'm hoping he's wrong."

"Maybe he's incompetent and this is all in his head," she offered.

"Well," Clint said, "at the very least, he hasn't thrown me in the brig and I'm getting a free passage to Sydney."

"So you're not mad, anymore?"

"I admit, I'm having second thoughts about agreeing to come with you, but no, I'm not mad."

"Good," she said, "when we get to Sydney we can still make this an adventure."

"And the Outback?"

"That, too," she agreed.

"Let me get back to these men before they shoot each other," Clint said.

"I'm going to get something to eat," she said. "Somebody never brought me breakfast."

"Sorry about that," Clint said. "I guess I got too involved."

"That's okay," she said. "I'll see you later. You can make it up to me tonight."

"By bringing you dinner," he said.

"Sure," she said, "that, too."

Chapter Fifteen

Clint spent the rest of the afternoon with the men, until they ran out of plates. One of the men assured him that the cook said there were cups, mugs and saucers still available. Clint thought they would be useful if he decided to use smaller targets.

He sent all the weapons back to the main armory with Rory and Silas, with orders to clean them, again. The other men he dismissed.

While the passengers dispersed once the target practice was over, he noticed a man still standing there, watching. He recognized him as Ben Wheeler, the Australian. He walked over and Wheeler smiled.

"What's all the target practice about?"

Clint made a quick decision.

"Buy me a drink and I'll tell you."

"It's a deal, mate. Come on."

They went to the bar. It looked like half of the dispersed passengers had also gone there. They found spots at the bar and Wheeler ordered two mugs of cold beer.

"So what's going on?" he asked.

"We're getting some men ready in case we run into a case of piracy."

"Pirates? You mean, like, Jolly Roger pirates?"

"I don't know if they'll be flying a flag, but the Captain's heard some scuttlebutt about it."

"Hey, mate," Wheeler said, "if you need help, I can shoot. I did my time in the Colonial Army, and I've had my battles with the Bush Rangers."

"Bush Rangers? What are those?"

"Outlaws in the Outback," Wheeler said. "Anybody who has a ranch has to deal with them."

"I thought you only had to deal with Aborigines," Clint said.

"You do, but Aborigines can be dealt with on friendly terms. There are no such opportunities with Bush Rangers. They're similar to your Comancheros."

"Well, in that case I may be able to use you," Clint said.

"How did you get yourself involved in this?" Wheeler asked.

"I was recognized when I got on board, and somebody told the Captain. He's been hearing some piracy talk, and asked for my help."

"And you agreed to fight pirates?"

"There was a little more to it than that, but it's not important."

"Well, I'm in if you need me . . . and from what I saw today, you probably will."

"Why don't you meet me in the main salon tomorrow morning?" Clint asked. "You'll get breakfast, and I'll introduce you."

"Suits me," Wheeler said. He drank his beer down and slapped the mug down on the bar. "I'll see you then."

As Wheeler walked away, Louis came walking over.

"The Captain would like you to have dinner with him again, at his table," he said.

"Tell him I'm not available," Clint said. "I've ignored my lady friend long enough today."

"I understand," Louis said. "I'll tell him. Any other message? He's going to ask me how we're coming along."

"Tell him there's a lot to be done, but he should let me know if he hears anything else."

"I'll tell him."

As the purser started away Clint said, "Hey, Louis, have a beer with me."

"Sure," the man said, turning back.

Clint waved at the bartender for two more.

"Tell me something," he said, handing Louis a mug.

"Sure," Louis said. "What is it?"

"Tell me about the Captain."

"What do you want to know about him?"

"Some history."

"He's been a ship's Captain for a very long time," Louis said.

"A good one?"

Louis hesitated.

"I need to know what I'm dealing with, Louis. That means the Captain, too."

"He was a good Captain for a long time," Louis said. "At least, that's what I heard. He's been the Captain of the Princess for many years. I've been here only a few, and I'm looking for more."

"Why's that?"

"Let's just say it's because Captain Farmington was a good man for many years."

Clint took that to mean that Farmington was no longer considered a good Captain.

"I really don't want to say more than that," Louis added. He put the beer down, only half consumed. "Thanks for the drink."

"Sure thing."

As the purser walked away, Clint drank his beer and wondered if he had finally gotten himself in over his head.

Chapter Sixteen

"I've been waiting for you," Meg said, as Clint entered.

"I brought you a plate," Clint said, holding it aloft. "You can eat while I freshen up."

"I see two plates," she said.

"I'll join you once I've washed up."

"Good," she said, accepting the plates and setting them down on the table. "You can tell me what's been going on."

He used the pitcher-and-basin to wash up, and then sat at the table with her and started eating. He had brought two plates of stew back with him.

"I think I've gotten in over my head," he said.

"Why's that?"

"The men I've got aren't much good, and the Captain's not much better."

"What are you going to do?"

"I'll work with what I have. Meanwhile, I'll hope this piracy business is all in the Captain's head."

"And if it isn't?"

"We'll find out soon enough," Clint said. "Meanwhile, tell me about the Bush Rangers."

"Bush Rangers?" she repeated. "Where did you hear about them?"

"Ben Wheeler," Clint said. "He's offered his services, said he's had experience fighting Bush Rangers."

"Anybody with a station has dealt with them," she said.

"He said they're like Comancheros."

"That sounds right," Meg said.

"Are they thieves or killers?" Clint asked.

"A little bit of both, I'd say," Meg replied. "But you're not going to encounter any of them out here."

"I figure Bush Rangers sound as bad as pirates."

"You're probably right."

"Then Wheeler would be a good man to have on my side."

"I don't know him, but that sounds right, too," she said.

"Now all I need is another dozen like him."

"What about the passengers?" she asked. "There must be some good men among them."

"But any talk of piracy is likely to panic them."

"So what're you going to do?"

"Work with what I've got, I guess," Clint answered. "Like I said, this may all be in the Captain's head."

"I hope you're right. This stew is pretty good."

"Eat it all," he said." You're going to need your strength for what comes next."

"Yum," she said, with a smile.

***

They went to bed after dinner.

True to his word, Meg needed all her strength to keep up with him.

He fucked her missionary style until they were both covered with sweat, then flipped her over onto her belly and took her that way, pounding in-and-out of her for a good long while until he erupted a hot geyser of semen into her.

After a few minutes of rest she reached down for his cock and stroked it until he was hard again.

"Wow, you weren't kidding about needing my strength," she said.

"You done?" he asked.

"Not hardly," she said, gripping him tightly, "and I can see you're not, either."

She moved down between his legs and wasted no time taking him into her mouth and sucking. She stayed with him as he started to buck, and finally exploded . . .

***

"I need a break," she said.

"Brandy?" he asked.

"Sounds good."

He padded naked into the other room, poured two brandies and brought them back to bed. She sat with her back against the headboard and sipped. He studied her nipples with great pleasure as he drank.

"I get the feeling this is a quick little down payment," Meg said.

"On what?"

"On some more time spent on my own while you build your little army."

"I think of it as more of a navy," he said.

She waved her hand.

"Same thing."

"I could be in the brig, and you'd be alone."

"Oh, believe me," she said, "I fully understand. I'm the one who sneaked you on board, so I have to stay. Just do me a favor."

"What's that?" he asked.

"Don't get yourself killed."

"Believe me," he told her, taking her glass so he could fill it again, "that's my plan."

Chapter Seventeen

The next morning Clint found Ben Wheeler in the salon with the other men. It seemed he had already introduced himself and was eating with some of them. Clint got himself a plate and joined them.

"Good morning," he said to all of them.

The sailors at the table grumbled back a good morning, but Ben Wheeler smiled and said, "I met some of the fellas when I first got on the ship."

"Well, enjoy your breakfast and then I'll introduce you to all the others."

"Are we going to do some shooting today?" Wheeler asked.

"We are," Clint said, "smaller targets."

The other men groaned.

"What about hand-to-hand?" Wheeler asked.

"Is that something you're good at?" Clint asked.

"I was a wrestler, as a young man. I think I can show them a thing or two."

"That's a good idea, Ben," Clint said. "I'll give you some of these beefy fellas to work with."

"Suits me."

Clint ate his breakfast quickly, then stood in the center of the room.

"This is Ben Wheeler," he announced, "one of your passengers. Stand up, Ben."

Ben stood and tipped his hat.

"I'm going to have Ben school some of you in hand-to-hand combat. If any of you feel you don't need schooling, come and see me. But only if you're a fighter, not a brawler. The rest of you will be shooting again, but this time at smaller targets, saucers and cups." A groan went up in the room. "Don't worry," Clint said, "some of you will hit them. I guarantee it. Finish your breakfast. We're going out on deck in fifteen minutes."

This time when Clint sat at a table it was with Silas and Rory.

"How are the guns?" he asked.

"Oiled and ready," Rory assured him.

"Okay," Clint said, "go bring them out. We'll be there in ten."

"Gotcha."

Rory and Silas stood up and left the salon. Clint looked around, saw Louis sitting alone, eating, and joined him with a cup of coffee.

" 'morning, Louis."

"Mr. Adams."

"I think it's time you started calling me Clint, don't you?"

"Well, Mr. Adams," he said, "I take my job very seriously, and as purser of the Princess, need to treat my passengers with the proper respect. So, if you don't mind . . ."

"No, that's fine," Clint said. "How did the Captain react to my refusal of his dinner invitation."

"To tell you the truth," Louis said, "I think he missed dining with the lady more."

"I don't blame him. Did you tell him I was asking about him?"

"Well," Louis said, "he is my Captain."

"I understand."

"But as long as you continue to train the men, he said he's willing to answer any questions you may have, himself."

"I'll keep that in mind," Clint said. "You ready for today?"

"I am."

"And what about your regular duties as purser."

"I've delegated them."

"Then let's go."

They all stood and filed out of the salon. As they reached the deck, Ben Wheeler took off his jacket and shirt to reveal a muscular upper body.

Clint listened to what some of the men had to say, and delegated four of them to go with Wheeler, while the others took part in the shooting.

He tried to teach the men not to aim, but to point at what they wanted to hit. To demonstrate, he had two men throw saucers out into the air, the way they had tossed plates the day before. With two quick shots, he shattered both saucers. He then had the men do the same with two mugs, and also shattered them. After that he replaced the rounds in his gun, and holstered it. He then did the same thing with a rifle.

"You'll notice I never took the time to aim," Clint said, "I just pointed and pulled the trigger. That's what I want all of you to do. Rory, put them through some paces. I want to check on Wheeler."

"Yes, Sir."

"While the shooting went on behind him Clint walked to another section of the deck, where Wheeler was working with the four men. The shooting and wrestling had both attracted passengers as observers. Clint wondered if any of Captain Farmington's pirates were in the crowd?

Chapter Eighteen

The more time that passed with Clint working the men—with Ben Wheeler's help—piracy seemed less of a possibility. On occasion, Clint agreed to have a dinner for him and Meg with the Captain. The more time he spent talking to the man, the more he figured the threat was in his head. But at least Clint working the men made him happy, and kept Clint out of the brig.

Clint and Meg began taking all their meals in the dining room. Their evenings were spent in bed, and Clint realized this was the longest relationship he had ever had with a woman, and there were still months to come. He had never expected to be with a woman this long, but the extended time together wasn't a problem. They were still enjoying each other's company. He just hoped that, when he decided to go back to the states, Meg wouldn't be looking for anything permanent. He was to set in his ways for that.

He spent some time in the bar in the evenings, talking with some of the men, including Ben Wheeler, who he had started to think of as a friend.

Two weeks out of Sydney the Captain once again sent a dinner invitation, but this time it was only for Clint.

"What do you think is on his mind?" Meg asked. "Pirates?"

"I hope not," Clint said. "I was starting to think we were going to get to Sydney without having to deal with that."

"Well," she said, "I'll wait in the cabin like a good little girl, and you can bring me a plate."

He wasn't thrilled by the wifely tone, but he let it go.

***

The men had dispersed after another workout when Ben Wheeler came over, wiping his bare torso with a towel.

"I have to clean up, but how about dinner?" he asked.

"Sorry, the Captain beat you to it. He invited me without Meg."

"What do you think is on his mind?" Wheeler asked. "Pirates?"

"I'm hoping not."

"Well, would you like me to take the lovely lady to dinner?"

"I don't think so," Clint said. "I trust you with the men but not with my woman."

Wheeler laughed and said, "I don't blame you. I'll see you in the bar, later."

Wheeler went to his cabin, and Clint made for the dining room.

***

When he reached the Captain's table the man was sitting there alone.

"Thank you for coming," Farmington said, rising to shake hands. "I hope the lady wasn't offended."

"Not at all," Clint said.

The Captain waited until they had ordered to get to the point.

"I'm sure you're wondering why I invited only you," he said.

"I am, indeed."

"We're two weeks out of Sydney," Farmington said. "If it's going to happen, it'll happen soon."

"Why now?" Clint asked. "Why wouldn't they have hit us further out to sea?"

"I think after they strike, they'd want to get to shore quickly," the man said.

"But you haven't heard anything?" Clint said.

"No," the Captain said, "not since the first time, a few weeks out of New York."

"They're not going to be able to just pull up along-side and board us," Clint said. "I have men with guns watching both sides."

"Port and starboard," Farmington corrected.

"Yes, right."

"I'm assuming they already have men on board, either passengers or crew."

"Hopefully I haven't put guns in the hands of planted pirates," Clint said.

"I can vouch for the men I gave you," Farmington said.

"All of them?"

"I've worked with my men a long time."

"No exceptions?"

The Captain thought a moment, then said, "Only one."

"Who's that?"

"My purser."

"Louis?"

Farmington nodded.

"Why him?"

"He's the youngest member of my crew," Farmington said.

"But hasn't he been here for years?"

"A few years," Farmington said. "That's nothing when you're a member of a crew."

Chapter Nineteen

Louis wasn't in the dining room, so Clint asked the Captain where his cabin was.

"What for?"

"I want to talk to him," Clint said. "You just gave me an idea."

Farmington gave him directions to the cabin.

"If he's not there, you might want to try the telegraph room."

"You can get telegrams while you're out to sea?"

"As long as we're not too far out," Farmington said.

"What about from another nearby boat?"

"Sure."

"And if you can be contacted by another boat, can you see it?"

"Not necessarily."

Clint stood up.

"Don't you want to finish your dinner?"

"I'll come back to get a plate for Meg," Clint said. "But now I've got two ideas."

"Well," the Captain said, "let me know what you're up to."

"You'll be the first to know."

***

Clint knocked on the door of Louis' cabin. When Louis opened the door he stiff-armed him, driving him back several steps before he fell on his butt.

"What the hell—what'd you do that for?"

"Because I got an idea about you, boy," Clint said, entering the cabin and closing the door behind him.

"Louis started to get up, but Clint yelled, "Stay down!"

Louis looked at him, then sat back down.

"What's on your mind, Mr. Adams?"

"You're the youngest and newest member of the Princess' crew," Clint said. "You know what that makes me think?"

Louis' shoulders slumped.

"I've got a good idea."

"Tell me you're not part of the pirate crew that intends to take this ship."

"We ain't pirates."

"So you admit it?"

"Sure," Louis said, "I'm part of a group who intends to rescue this ship from Captain Farmington."

"You better explain that statement to me," Clint said.

"Can I get up?"

"No!"

"This was once one of the finest ships on the ocean," Louis said. "My father was the Captain, until he died."

"And then what?"

"And then Farmington took it over, and he's run it into the ground with a piss poor crew and no skill at all as a captain."

"You told me he was a good Captain once."

"I lied," Louis said. "He's the worst ship's captain who ever lived."

"So you're going it take it back?"

"I am."

"You and your men?"

"Me and my colleagues."

"And when is this going to happen?"

"It was going to happen on this trip," Louis said.

"Not anymore?"

"No."

"What changed you mind?"

"You did," Louis said. "Neither I nor my colleagues want anything to do with you, Mr. Adams. So you disembark when we get to Sydney, and mind your own business."

"So you and your . . . colleagues, you'll take her on her way back to New York?"

"That's about the size of it."

"What about the men I've been training?"

"They won't be worth spit without you," Louis said, "you know that."

"How old are you, Louis?"

"I'm thirty."

"You want to get any older?"

Louis smiled.

"You won't kill me," he said. "I'm unarmed."

Clint hated that the young man was right.

"I'll tell the Captain what you have in mind," Clint said, "and you'll be off your Princess."

"I'll still take 'er," Louis said.

"You got any more men on board?"

Louis laughed.

"One," he said. "The radio operator. That's how I sent my people a message that you were on board. They agreed we should call everything off while you're here."

"What's all this horseshit about pirates?"

"Louis laughed again.

"I started that rumor, just to scare Farmington. But I didn't expect him to rope you in on this."

"Who recognized me getting on board?" Clint asked.

"I did," Louis said. "I saw you once when I was a kid, in St. Louis. I was stupid enough to tell the Captain. I thought he'd toss you in the brig."

"I guess he's not so dumb then," Clint said.

Louis shrugged.

"So he made one smart move in his life," he said. "It's gonna do him no good when you're done."

"He's going to put you and your man off in Sydney, Louis," Clint said, "and then he'll be ready for you and your friends."

"He'll be no match for us," Louis said. "They're gonna be the new crew of the Sea Princess, and they'll be a good one."

"And you'll be the new captain?"

"Hell, no, I'm no sea captain," Louis said. "I got one picked out."

"So what do you get out of it?"

"I told you," Louis said, "I'm rescuing the old scow to make a fine lady out of her, again."

Clint thought it over for a moment.

"Okay, get up and put your boots on."

Louis got to his feet, sat on a chair and started pulling on his boots.

"What've you got in mind?"

"We're going to see your friend, the radio operator."

Louis stood up, looking tense.

"Don't try anything, Louis," Clint said.

"Don't worry," Louis said, "I'm not giving you an opportunity to shoot me."

"I'm not going to kill you, but I can't speak for the Captain."

Chapter Twenty

A half hour later they were standing in the Captain's quarters. Clint had Louis and the radio operator, Bob Spikes, standing in front of Captain Farmington.

"Louis?" Farmington said to Clint. "He's behind this?"

"He started the rumor about pirates," Clint said. "There's a ship out there with his friends on it."

"No pirates?" the older man asked.

"Just a band of men who want your ship," Clint said. "Maybe a hundred years ago they might have been flying a Jolly Roger. Now they're just a bunch of men with guns."

Farmington looked at Louis.

"Is this true, boy?"

"It's true, you broken down old man," Louis said.

"What was your father's name?"

"Captain James Olcott," Louis said. "I'm Louis Olcott."

Captain Farmington looked at Clint.

"It's true, Olcott was the Captain before me. Before he drank himself to death."

"You're a liar!" Louis shouted. He lunged forward, but Clint grabbed him and pulled him back.

"What about Spikes?" Clint asked.

"I hired him on Louis' word," Farmington said. "Are you sure these are the only two on board."

"Not a hundred-per-cent," Clint said. "I don't know how they planned on taking the ship with only two of them on board, but it's possible."

"I had a plan," Louis said.

"What plan?" Farmington asked.

Louis laughed.

"I ain't tellin' you."

Farmington looked at Spikes.

"What about you?"

Spikes shrugged.

"Louis calls the play. I just work the radio."

Farmington looked at Clint.

"Well," he said, "I asked you to find pirates on my boat and kill them. How do you want to do it? Shoot 'em, or make 'em walk the plank?"

"You can't do that!" Spikes said. "I'll tell ya what I know, but I don't know much. I tol' ya, I just worked the radio."

"Oh, now you're talking like a pirate," Clint said. "I'm not about to kill two unarmed men. You'll have to do that yourself."

Farmington stared at the two men, then looked back at Clint. His shoulders slumped.

"I'm no killer," he said. "Whataya suggest I do with 'em? Set them adrift in a dingy?"

"They'll be picked up by their friends," Clint said. "Then you'll have to watch out for them."

"So what do I do?"

"Well," Clint said, "I'll tell you . . ."

***

"What did you tell him to do with them?" Meg asked, while she ate the plate of food Clint brought her.

"Right now they're both in the brig," Clint said. "When we get to Sydney I suggested he turn them over to the law." Clint frowned. "They do have law in Sydney, don't they?"

"I believe so," she said. "What about the other men, out there in a boat?"

"They're not going to know what to do if they never hear from Louis, again."

"They won't come after the ship?"

"It was all Louis' idea," Clint said. "If they don't hear from him ever again, they're likely to believe he's at the bottom of the ocean."

"So you saved the day after all, and didn't need to train all those men."

"Not at all."

"And what's the Captain going to do for you?"

"He offered me my own cabin."

"Did you take it?"

"Of course not," Clint said, "but I did get him to agree to return your passage fare."

"Well then," she said, grabbing her wine glass, "that deserves a toast, doesn't it?"

Clint picked up a glass and said, "I believe it does."

Chapter Twenty-One

As it turned out, Ben Wheeler was a big help with the Australian police.

"When we get to Sydney," he told Clint, "I can call for some constables to come and pick up Louis and the other fella."

"You have those kind of connections?" Clint asked.

"I know some people," Wheeler said. "I don't know what the police will do with them, I don't think Australia has any laws governing piracy. They might just want to ship them back to the states and let your Navy take care of them."

"Anything will work," Clint said. "I'd just like to keep Louis from contacting his people. That should keep them confused."

"I assume you'll be heading to New South Wales by rail," Wheeler said. "That's where Miss McGregor's property is."

"That's up to Meg," Clint said. "I'm just along for the ride. I believe there's a lawyer she needs to see."

"Well then," Wheeler said, "I'll say goodbye and wish you luck." They shook hands.

"Where's your ranch?" Clint asked, before Wheeler could walk away.

"It's also in New South Wales."

"So we might be seeing each other again," Clint surmised.

"It's possible," Wheeler said, "but the Outback is big country."

"What kind of law do they have out there?"

"Law enforcement these days is usually made up of Aboriginal soldiers, led by white officers. And I have to say, they're almost as bad as the bush rangers their chasing."

"Are the bush rangers very active?"

"The police hung Ned Kelly some years ago. He was the worst of them, but they're still out there."

"Ned Kelly?"

"Some considered him a Robin Hood," Wheeler said, "but others saw him as a vicious killer. He was hung for killing policemen."

"Sounds pretty bad."

"Don't be confused," Wheeler said. "Things are getting pretty modernized in Australia, but there are still areas that are pretty wild. I hope everything goes well for you and Meg."

As Wheeler started to walk away, Clint saw some uniformed police approaching and stopping to speak with

Captain Farmington. He didn't want to get more involved, so he walked away, to meet with Meg, who was
waiting on the dock. But as he walked, he wondered just
when Ben Wheeler put out his call for the police?

***

Clint and Meg got her luggage loaded onto a wagon
that took them to the Royal Sydney Hotel.

"When are you supposed to meet with this lawyer?"
he asked.

"Well," she said, "we arrived on time, so it should be
tomorrow."

"How will we be getting to this property you inherited?"

"By rail."

"How long of a ride is it?"

"About six hundred kilometers."

"How many miles is that?"

"Oh, sorry." She smiled, a bit chagrined. "I'm already falling back into my Australian upbringing. That's
about three hundred and eighty miles, to you, mate." She
smiled again.

"Seven or eight hours on a train?" he said.

"Not so bad after three months on a ship."

"And when we arrive?"

"We'll have to get some horses," she said. "It'll still be about a hundred miles into the Outback."

"What about Aborigines and bush rangers?" Clint asked.

"You've been doing your research," she said. "We'll just have to hope we don't run into them."

"Can we get a police escort?"

"Those local soldiers are just as bad," she said.

"Why would you want to live out there?"

"Why did people want to live on Indian land in the states?" she asked. "Sometimes you don't have a choice where your home is."

When they reached the hotel a couple of dark skinned boys came out to grab their luggage.

"Aborigines?" Clint asked.

"Yes," she said, "but more civilized."

They followed the boys in. Meg registered and got their key.

"One room?" he asked.

"Is that a problem?" she asked.

"Not for me."

The ride from the docks to the hotel through the Sydney streets showed a growing city. The Royal Sydney Hotel looked to have recently been constructed.

The boys dropped the luggage to the floor and Clint tipped them before sending them away. It was one large room with a large bed, two chairs, and a chest of drawers with a pitcher-and-basin on it.

"It's not so different," he commented.

"What did you expect?" she asked, taking off her shawl. "I want to get out of this dress."

"Already?" he asked, sitting on the bed.

She laughed and said, "I want to get something to eat. And for the rest of the time, I'll be in pants, if that doesn't offend you."

"Not in the least," he assured her, with a smile.

Chapter Twenty-Two

When they got back downstairs Clint looked around the lobby.

"No dining room?"

"New South Wales is becoming modernized," she said, "but slowly. We'll find a restaurant down the street."

They went out the front door and turned left.

"Sydney's in New South Wales?" he asked.

"Yup."

"And so's the Outback your property is in? Is there any Federal law?"

"According to the telegrams I received, not yet," she said. "We're still dealing with Colonial enforcement. In the Outback that means drafting men in from the local Aboriginal tribes."

"And that's why one's as bad as the other?"

"You got it, mate."

They reached a place called The Sand Hook Café.

"Let's go in here," she said.

"Is it good?"

"Damned if I know," she said. "I've been away a long time, but it's probably as good as any."

They stepped inside and a waiter came rushing up.

"Take any table you want, folks," he said. "It's too early for the rush."

"The back," Clint said to Meg.

"We could sit by the window," she said. "Nobody's going to take a shot at you here."

"Old habits die hard," he told her. "The back."

"Of course."

They walked and sat at a table against the back wall.

"You folks want a menu?" the older waiter asked.

"Do you have sausage sizzle?" Meg asked.

"We sure do, Ma'am."

She looked at Clint.

"I told you I've been away a long time," she said. "Sausage sizzle is good."

"What is it?"

"Pretty much just a sausage sandwich," she said, "but you can heap it with lots of sauces and mustards."

"Let's do it, then."

"And beer?"

"God, yes," he said.

She looked at the waiter and said, "Two sausage sizzles and two beers."

"Coming up," he said.

As the waiter went to the kitchen Meg said, "You know, when we get situated, I can cook for you. I'm a damn good cook, just never had time to do it in the U.S."

"Sounds good," he said.

"Don't look so nervous," she said. "I'm not looking for a husband. I'm happy with what we're doing, and I know you'll be heading home soon."

"Not so soon," he said. "Sounds like we've got a ways to go."

"I know you've already had to deal with more than you bargained for," she said. "After we talk to the lawyer tomorrow, I could go on to the Outback by myself, and you could take the next ship home. I'm sure there's one other than the Princess."

"Hey, I've come all this way," Clint said. "I'd like to see the Outback and this property of yours."

She smiled broadly.

"I'm glad to hear you say that," she said. "I just wanted to give you an out."

"And I appreciate it," he said, "but I'll let you know when I've had enough."

They stopped talking as the waiter came out with plates and mugs, amazingly balancing it all up and down his arms. He set everything down on the table, backed up and said, "I will bring sauces. You can choose your own."

Clint looked at the sausage sizzle, unsure as to whether it was beef or pork. But it looked good, sitting between two pieces of thick bread.

"It's pork," she said.

The waiter came back with several saucers filled with red and brown sauces.

"Try this one," Meg said, taking the red and pouring it over her sandwich.

"I think I'll try this one," Clint said, doing the same with the brown.

They both picked up their sandwich and took a big bite.

"It's very good," Clint said to her.

"I told you," she said, chewing hers. There was red sauce smeared around her mouth, and she wiped it with a napkin. Clint did the same, then took another bite, washing it down with cold beer.

"That's good, too," he said.

"Australian beer is the best," Meg said.

"I won't argue with you."

They then turned all their attention to their food, wolfing it down hungrily.

Chapter Twenty-Three

The bed in the room was large and comfortable. They bounced around on it for a while, but eventually gave in to the fatigue of the ocean crossing, and fell asleep.

They woke the next morning with bright sunlight coming through the window.

"Well, you're home," Clint said.

"Yes, I am."

"How do you feel about it?"

"I won't really know until we get to the Outback," Meg said. "But first I need to talk to the lawyer about my options."

"What do you consider your options are?"

"Keep the land or sell it."

"Why would you keep it?" Clint asked. "Can you grow anything on it?"

"In the Outback? Not much. But I could raise horses, and cattle."

"What do you know about doing that?"

"Not a damn thing," she said. "I'd need help."

He didn't respond.

"But there's somebody out there looking after things til I get there," she went on. "I'll talk with them."

"How many are there?"

"I don't know," she said. "Maybe the lawyer does."

A knock came at the door.

"You answer that," Clint said, grabbing his gun from the bedpost. He stood to one side while Meg donned a robe and went to the door. When she opened it, he saw the young desk clerk who had checked her in.

"Charles, isn't it?" she asked.

"Yes, Ma'am," the clerk said. "You remembered."

"What can I do for you, Charles?"

"There's a fella down at the desk who's askin' for you, Ma'am," Charles said. "He says he's your lawyer."

"Well," she said, "you tell him we'll be down momentarily."

"We?"

"Mr. Adams and me," she said.

"He only asked for you, Ma'am."

She smiled, stroked his cheek, which made him blush, and said, "Just tell 'im."

"Yes, Ma'am."

She closed the door and stared at a naked Clint, standing there with his gun.

"Well, it looks like we're about to get some answers."

***

When Clint and Meg came down to the lobby a tall, well-dressed man in his fifties was standing at the front desk, waiting.

"Miss McGregor?" he asked.

"Yes, Sir," she said. "And this is my friend, Mr. Adams."

"Mr. Adams." The lawyer shook his hand. "I heard what happened on your ship during your crossing. Seems you averted a lot of bloodshed."

"I had help."

"My name is Alan Carstairs, Attorney-at-Law."

"Mr. Carstairs notified me by wire and sent me the money for the crossing."

"I represented Miss McGregor's uncle, Frank McGregor," Carstairs said. "I adhered to his wishes. Shall we go someplace where we can talk?"

"How about your office?" Clint said.

Carstairs looked at him indignantly and said, "I was speaking to the lady."

"Mr. Adams will be part of any discussions we have," Meg said.

"I see. Very well. There's a fine saloon just down the street. May I buy you each a drink?"

"By all means," Meg said.

***

It might have been a natural dislike of lawyers, one that the profession had well earned from Clint, but he didn't like Alan Carstairs. There was something about the man's tone that rubbed him the wrong way.

He and Meg followed the lawyer to the saloon and entered. At midday it was only doing a modest business.

"I'll get the drinks," Carstairs said, "you folks pick out a table."

As with the café, Clint chose a back table. Carstairs turned with the drinks, looked around and seemed surprised when he saw where they were sitting.

When he brought the drinks over he said, "I thought we might sit near the window."

"I don't like windows," Meg said, quickly. "I like this one."

Carstairs looked at Clint and said, "The lady has a mind of her own." He sat down.

"You don't know the half of it, Mr. Carstairs," Clint said. "You might as well just have a seat. And start talking."

Chapter Twenty-Four

"I don't know what your intentions are, Miss McGregor," Carstairs said, "but I brought some papers along in case you just wanted to sell the property. You'd just have to sign it over."

"Sign it over to who?" Clint asked. "You?"

"Well," Carstairs said, "I thought that would be most prudent. I didn't want the lady to have to spend more time on this than need be."

"You said her uncle wanted her to have the property," Clint said.'

"Well, yes," Carstairs said, "but it's in the Outback. That's no place for a lady."

"I would think that'd be my decision to make, Mr. Carstairs," Meg said, "don't you?"

"Well, yes, of course," Carstairs said. "I was just trying to be—"

"—prudent?" Clint finished.

"Exactly."

"I think I'd like to look my property over before I decide what to do with it," Meg said. "That would be the most prudent thing to me."

"Of course, of course," Carstairs said. "Pardon my impertinence." He took some papers from his coat pocket and set them on the table. "I'll just leave the papers with you to peruse. If you need any help with the legal aspects, my office address is included." He sipped his beer and left most of it as he stood. "Good day, for now."

"Mr. Carstairs," Meg said, "we're probably going to take the train out there tomorrow."

"I see. Well, you'll have to get off in Parramatta Junction, but that will still be a distance for you to travel on horseback, or by buggy. But I'm sure you'll find a telegraph office there, so just contact me when you've decided." He touched the brim of his hat. "Madam." He looked at Clint, but made no gesture and just left.

"I don't like him," Meg said.

"Good girl."

***

Alan Carstairs was seething as he walked back to his office. When he entered, Edward Hopkins was there.

"Well?" he asked.

"That bitch!" He threw his hat across the room and sat at his desk.

"No pushover?" Hopkins asked.

"Not at all. What did you find out about this Adams character?"

"His name's Clint Adams," Hopkins said. "He's known in the West as the Gunsmith."

"A gunman?"

"Definitely."

"With a reputation?"

"One Ned Kelly would've been proud of."

"How many men has he gunned down?" Carstairs asked. "Or does he shoot them in the back?"

"Oh, no," Hopkins said. "He guns them down, but doesn't count, and apparently nobody else has."

"A gunman from the West who doesn't put notches on his gun?" Carstairs asked. "This man is going to be a problem."

"If we get rid of him," Hopkins said, "do you think she'll fall in line?"

"No," Carstairs said, "she has a mind of her own. We're going to have to push."

"When do we start?"

"Let's give her some time to get there," Carstairs said. "You have some men ready."

"Bush rangers, or Aborigines?"

"We might need both."

***

Clint and Meg walked back to the hotel and went to their room before unfolding the papers the lawyer had given them.

"Is this all the property was worth?" Clint asked, after looking them over.

"Hardly," she said. "It's a fraction."

"Carstairs was trying to pull a fast one," Clint said.

"I told you I didn't like him." She slumped in her chair. "He brought me all this way just to try to cheat me?"

Clint dropped the papers on the table and sat back in the other chair. "I think you're going to have to hire a lawyer of your own, Meg."

"How?"

"You're not likely to find one in the Outback, are you?" he asked.

"I don't think so."

"Then you're going to need to get a recommendation from somebody."

"But who?"

Clint gave it a moment's thought, then said, "I think I might have someone in mind."

Chapter Twenty-Five

"Ben Wheeler?" Meg repeated. "Do you even know where he is?"

"Well, he's in Sydney, preparing to go to his own property in the Outback," Clint said. "All I have to do is find him. After all, he offered to help."

"Where are you going to look?"

"If he's not in this hotel," Clint said, "what hotel do you think he would be in?"

"From what you've said about him, he would be in the best."

"I'll check the register downstairs and see if he's here," Clint said. "If he's not, the desk clerk can steer me to the next best hotel."

"I'll come with you," she said. "Charles is sweet on me. He'll give me all the help he can."

"Let's go, then," Clint said.

***

Down in the lobby, Charles saw them coming and straightened his back, and his suit and tie.

"Miss McGregor," he greeted, "what can I do for you and your gentleman friend?"

"We would like to take a look at your register, Charles," Meg said. "We're looking for a friend."

"Well, Ma'am, if you tell me who he is, I'll tell you if he's here."

"His name is Ben Wheeler."

"Mr. Wheeler is not registered in our establishment," Charles said, "but I can tell you where he is."

"You know him?" Clint asked.

"Mr. Wheeler is quite well known," Charles said. "You'll find him registered in The Commonwealth House, about two blocks east of here. It's the second-best hotel in Sydney."

"After this one?" Clint asked.

"Of course."

"I wonder why he's not staying here?" Clint said.

"He and the owner don't get along," Charles said.

"Thank you, Charles," Meg said.

"My pleasure, Ma'am."

Clint and Meg left the hotel and started walking east.

***

They found the Commonwealth House with no trouble. On the basis of appearance, Clint would have guessed the Commonwealth as the best hotel in Sydney. Perhaps there were other, unseen attributes in the Royal Sydney.

They presented themselves at the front desk and asked for Ben Wheeler's room number.

"Mr. Wheeler doesn't like us to just give out his room number," the clerk said, "Can I tell him who's askin' for him?"

"Clint Adams and Meg McGregor."

"Please wait here," the clerk said. He left the desk and went up the staircase. When he came back down moments later, he positioned himself behind the desk again before speaking.

"Mr. Wheeler is in room one, at the top of the stairs. He's invited you to go up."

"Thank you," Clint said. He and Meg started for the stairs, but Clint stopped and turned. "By the way, Mr. Wheeler wouldn't happen to own this hotel, would he?"

"Oh, no, Sir," the clerk said, "Edward Hopkins is the owner."

Clint nodded, took Meg's arm and led her up the stairs. At room one they knocked on the door. It was opened by a smiling Ben Wheeler.

"Clint, and Miss McGregor. How nice to see you both. Come on in."

They entered and found themselves in a high-ceilinged, well-furnished room that seemed to be the front part of a two room suite.

"Nice digs," Clint commented.

"Can I offer you a drink? Whiskey? Brandy?"

Meg looked at Clint, who said, "Not right now."

"Then tell me what I can do for you."

"We met with the lawyer who brought Meg here. He wasted no time trying to cheat her out of her inheritance."

"What's his name?"

"Alan Carstairs."

"I'm not surprised."

"You know him?"

"He's a cheater from way back."

"Well, Meg needs a lawyer of her own, one she can trust."

"That's not an easy task," Wheeler said. "You can hardly trust any lawyer."

"Well," Clint said, "I was hoping you'd be able to recommend one."

Wheeler poured himself a brandy and drank it down.

"I'll have to give it some thought," he said. "Join me here for dinner in two hours. I might have something for you by then."

"Dinner here?"

"Yes, the Commonwealth has a small dining room downstairs. Let's say seven?"

"We'll be here."

As they left it seemed to Clint that the Commonwealth definitely had some attributes the Royal did not.

Chapter Twenty-Six

Clint and Meg went back to their hotel and killed two hours the best way they knew how. When they were lying in each others exhausted arms, Meg asked, "Do you think Mr. Wheeler will be able to help?"

"I can almost guarantee it," Clint said.

"You know him better than I do."

"I don't think I know him at all," Clint said, "but, strangely enough, I trust him."

"Why?"

"He didn't have to offer his help on the ship," Clint said, "but he did. He whipped some of those men into fighting shape."

"Well," she said, "luckily all we need right now is a recommendation."

"I think an invitation to dinner might get us more than that," Clint said. "So we'd better get dressed and go to dinner."

***

The desk clerk at the Commonwealth greeted them with a smile.

"Mr. Wheeler is waiting in the dining room. This way, please."

He led them to a room that had five tables in it. Only one was occupied, by Wheeler and another man. They both stood as Clint and Meg approached. The man with Wheeler was well-dressed, short, stout, in his fifties. The table was set for four.

"Clint Adams and Meg McGregor," Wheeler said, "this is Randall Kingman, Attorney-at-Law."

"What a pleasure to meet you both," Kingman said, in an accent that was both British and Australian.

Clint shook the man's pudgy, damp hand.

"Mr. Kingman came here from England years ago and decided to stay. "Please, let's all be seated."

They all sat down.

"I understand you've had some dealings with Alan Carstairs," Kingman said.

"Do you know him?" Clint asked.

"I know him, and know of him," Kingman said. "He is a sad representative of our profession, I must say. I'm terribly sorry that you have become involved with him."

"And you're more upstanding?" Meg asked.

"Well," Kingman said, "a lawyer is a lawyer, but why don't we eat dinner and talk, and you can decide for yourself?"

"That sounds good to me," Meg said. "Clint?"

"Fine. Let's eat."

***

Wheeler, Clint and Meg ordered Wagyu steaks, while the pudgy lawyer, Kingman, ordered a large meat pie.

"This is my favorite of the local cuisine," he told Clint. "You should try it while you're here."

"I may do that."

"So, Miss McGregor," Kingman said, "tell me about your dealings the Carstairs."

"I inherited some property in the Outback from my uncle . . ." she started and went on to tell the lawyer everything.

"Do you have the paperwork with you?" he asked.

"I certainly do." She took it from her drawstring bag and passed it all over to him. He leafed through it while he continued to eat.

"Ah, yes," he said, passing it all back, "I can see Mr. Carstairs is up to his old tricks."

"He's done this before?" Clint asked.

"Many times."

"Am I stuck with him as my lawyer?" Meg asked.

"Not at all," Kingman said. "You are entitled to fire a lawyer any time you want. That includes Carstairs, or me."

"How do I do that?" she asked.

"Well," Kingman said, picking up his napkin and wiping his mouth, "you can start by hiring me, and then I will, in turn, terminate Carstairs, and supersede him as your lawyer."

Meg looked at Clint, who gave her a slight nod.

"When will you be traveling to the Outback to see your property?" Kingman asked.

"Tomorrow."

"On an early train?"

"Yes."

"I can bring papers for you to sign to your hotel before you leave. Once you sign, I'll take care of Carstairs."

"And my property?"

"Well," Kingman said, "you're going to have to let me know what you want to do with it. I assume you'll either keep it or sell it."

"To you?" Meg asked.

"Good Lord, no," Kingman said. "I have no use for such property."

"Then why does Carstairs want it?" Clint asked. "Isn't that an odd thing for a lawyer to do?"

"It certainly is."

Chapter Twenty-Seven

They agreed to meet in the lobby of the Commonwealth the next morning to sign the papers. Kingman quoted his rates to Meg, which she and Clint thought were reasonable, and Kingman left, shaking hands with all of them.

"Well," Wheeler said, "I hope you'll be satisfied." He stood. "I'll take my leave."

"Are you taking the morning train also, Ben?" Meg asked.

"No," Wheeler said. "I still have some business here. I'll be taking a later one."

"Thank you for your help."

He left, advising them that the meal was on him.

Clint and Meg asked the waiter for some more coffee.

"So what do you think?" Meg asked.

"I think you made the right decision to sign with Kingman," Clint said, "and to let him deal with Carstairs. That way you're free to go and take a look at your inheritance."

"I think so, too," she said. "I think I'm going to have enough to deal with, when we get there."

"You'll do fine."

"So far I am, with your help, and Ben Wheeler's."

"You're making your own decisions," Clint pointed out. "And doing it quite well."

They finished their coffee and left.

***

On the way back to the Royal Sydney Hotel Meg insisted on buying Clint some new clothes. They found a men's store that was closing within minutes and picked up some shirts and jeans that would fit any circumstance. They thanked the proprietor for remaining open and left.

"You'll need a bag to put these clothes in."

"I can roll them up in my bedroll," Clint said. The bedroll was really the only thing he had in the way of luggage.

"Nonsense," she said. "We can fit your clothes in my trunk."

"That works for me," Clint said.

When they got back to their room Meg laid out her travel clothes for the next day, and a new shirt and jeans for Clint. The rest of the clothes were packed in her bags and trunk.

After that they sat in a chair and Clint poured after-dinner drinks.

"What now?" she asked. The look on his face made it obvious what he was thinking.

"I'd like to talk," he said.

"About what?"

"About anything you haven't told me, yet."

"You think I'm holding something back from you, Clint?" she asked.

"I don't know," he said. "Are you?"

She bit her bottom lip and then sipped her brandy.

"Well . . ."

"You know more about this inheritance than you're letting on," he offered. "Is that it?"

Her shoulders slumped.

"Yes," she said. "I lived there as a young girl, and left when my father died. I haven't been back since."

"How well did you know your uncle?"

"He lived on the station," she said. "It was our family's home."

"And now it's yours," Clint said. "Do you want it?"

"I don't know," she said. "I know I want to see it before I decide."

"Why would the lawyer, Carstairs, want it?" he asked.

"That I don't know."

"And why did you want me to think you didn't know what the inheritance was?"

"I—I'm not sure," she said. "I guess I thought if I seemed ignorant about it, or helpless, you'd agree to come with me."

"And I did," Clint said, "but not for those reasons."

"Then why?" she asked. "For the sex?"

He smiled.

"That's part of it," he replied, "but it's like you said from the start, it's an adventure. As it turns out, it's been a bigger adventure than I even imagined."

She raised her glass to him and said, "Here's to adventure, then."

He returned the gesture and said, "To adventure."

She drained her glass, stood up and said, "And now . . . to sex!"

He followed her to the bed.

***

Alan Carstairs looked up from his desk as Edward Hopkins entered his office.

"I don't like that look on your face," Carstairs said. "What is it?"

"The McGregor woman has hired another attorney," Hopkins said.

"How do you know this?"

"They had dinner at my place."

Carstairs sat back.

"Who is it?"

"Kingman."

"That fat Brit?" he said. "How did she meet him."

"Through Ben Wheeler," Hopkins said.

"That bastard!" Carstairs swore. "Why's he getting' involved in my business?"

Hopkins shrugged and said, "Because he's Ben Wheeler."

"Yes," Carstairs said, "Well, that only holds while he's alive."

"Kingman and Wheeler?"

Carstairs scowled and said, "Both!"

Chapter Twenty-Eight

The next morning, they had some of the Aborigine boys take their luggage down to the lobby, and waited there for the lawyer, Randall Kingman, to arrive. When he did he bid them both good-morning, and they sat at a desk in the lobby to sign the papers. Kingman handed Meg her copies and pocketed his own.

"When will you fire Carstairs" Meg asked him.

"As soon as possible," he promised. "By the time you get off the train, he will no longer represent you."

"Good."

"I look forward to hearing from you," Kingman said. "My address and telegraph information are on the papers. Mr. Adams." He touched his finger to his bowler hat.

"Mr. Kingman," Clint said. "Thank you."

After he left, Clint and Meg had the boys carry the luggage out to a wagon, and then headed for the Australian Railway Line.

***

At the station the bags were loaded onto the train. Clint and Meg boarded and got two seats in the passenger car. Meg sat by the window.

The trip would take about seven hours, give or take a water stop or two.

"After this how long a ride will it be?" Clint asked.

"A few hours."

"Are you going to want to rent a buggy?"

She laughed and said, "I can ride. Two horses would do."

"What kind of a place is this Parramatta Junction?"

"Last I saw it, it was kind of a backwater mud puddle," she said. "If it has a telegraph office like Carstairs said, I suppose it's grown."

"We'll need a packhorse for your bags."

"I'm hoping for some help," she told him.

"Something else you haven't told me?"

"Um, I might have some cousins."

He turned his head and looked at her.

"How many cousins?"

"A few," she said, "depending on how many of them are still alive."

"This is going to be an interesting family," he commented.

"I hope you're right."

"Are they going to be glad to see you?" Clint asked.

"I have no idea."

"Would any of these cousins be your late uncle's sons?" Clint asked.

"One or two."

"Then why did he leave the property to you?"

"That's a good question."

Clint turned his body in his seat to face her.

"Meg, did you ask me along because you're expecting these cousins to try and kill you?"

"No, of course not."

He stared at her.

"I mean," she went on, "I'm not *expecting* them to . . ."

***

The train ride was uneventful, which suited Clint, considering what the ocean voyage had been like. For her part, Meg dozed while Clint watched the Australian expanse go by. He even spotted what he thought was a kangaroo, but decided not to ask anyone.

They made a couple of water stops. During one, Clint and Meg stepped down to stretch their legs. Clint saw a pack of animals off in the distance. They appeared to be a pack of dogs in light ginger and tan, black and tan, and creamy white fur.

"What are those?" he asked.

"Dingos, wild dogs." Meg told him.

"Why do they call them dingos?"

"The name goes way back. I don't know where it comes from."

From the distance Clint couldn't really judge their size, but they didn't seem to be as large as wolves.

"They're very fast," Meg said, "and have amazing stamina."

"Are they dangerous?"

"They're wild," Meg said, "so they're dangerous. They've been known to carry human babies off into the Outback. The Aborigines try to kill them as soon as they see them."

Clint decided that the closest species he could come to compare them with was wolves.

Once they were back on the train, the movement of the car once again rocked Meg to sleep. Clint decided to lose his own eyes, although he never really dozed off. That would call for him to be completely relaxed, which was not something the Gunsmith could do, even in Australia.

When the conductor walked through, announcing their arrival in Parramatta, Meg opened her eyes and stared out the window.

"As I suspected," she said, "it's grown." She gathered herself together, and they stood. "Let's get this last leg of our trip over with."

Chapter Twenty-Nine

As they disembarked, their bags were set out onto the platform, in front of the stationhouse.

"None of this was here when I left," Meg said.

"It looks and smells fairly new," Clint admitted. "Let's find out where we can get some horses."

"Don't worry about the bags," Meg said, staring into the distance. "I think they might be taken care of."

Clint turned to see what Meg was looking at. A dust cloud that quickly gave way to what appeared to be a buckboard, and some riders.

"Cousins?" he asked.

"We'll see."

The buckboard reached the train station and stopped. It looked like they had brought one extra saddled mount, a good-looking dun.

Three men dismounted, and a woman dropped down from the buckboard seat. They all mounted the platform and walked toward Clint and Meg. As they reached them a big bear of a man came forward and grabbed Meg in a strong hug.

"Cousin!" he brayed, hugging her tightly.

"Easy Daniel," one of the others said. "You'll break 'er."

"No chance of that," Daniel said, putting her down. "She's a solid McGregor."

"Cousin Meg?" the girl asked.

Meg stared at the girl, then smiled and asked, "Katy?"

Katy's face broke into a beautiful smile. She appeared to be in her early twenties.

"My God," Meg said, hugging her, "were you even walking the last time I saw you?"

"Just about," Katy said, looking at Clint.

"Oh, this my friend, Clint Adams," Meg said. "These are my cousins: Katy, Daniel, Matthew and James."

"*I'm* James," the youngest one said.

"*I'm* Matthew," the other said, and they all shook hands.

"I have to admit," Meg said, "I didn't know what to expect. I didn't know if you'd all still be here."

"Where else would we be?" Matthew asked. He appeared to be the oldest of the quartet.

"But . . . if you're all here, why am I here?" she asked. "Why did Uncle Frank leave everything to me?"

"We can talk about this when we get home," James said. "Come on boys, get these bags on the buckboard."

"Meg, we only brought one extra horse. We didn't know you'd be bringin' . . . a friend."

"That's all right," she said. "I'll ride with Katy."

"The two women walked arm-in-arm to the buckboard. Clint followed Matthew to the extra horse, while James and Daniel loaded the bags onto the buckboard.

"So," Matthew said, in a challenging tone, "are you and Meg married? Gettin' married?"

"We're just friends," Clint said.

"You came all the way from America with her because you're friends?"

"Exactly," Clint said. "She didn't know what to expect, and thought she might need help."

"Why does your name sound familiar to me?"

"Damned if I know," Clint said, mounting the dun.

Meg's three male cousins surrounded the buckboard as they rode away from the station, leaving Clint to trail behind. It was just as well that no one was talking to him. He had a lot of thinking to do.

Since Meg had three strapping male cousins to help her, he didn't see any reason for him to stay around much longer than necessary. In fact, he could even have caught the next train back to Sydney, whenever that was. It just remained to be seen how well Meg was going to get along with these cousins, whose father apparently left everything to Meg.

Riding from the station to the property was much like riding across the Mohave Desert, for Clint. He occasionally saw a kangaroo hopping in the distance. One even appeared to be fleeing from a pack of dingos.

Matthew dropped back eventually, to ride alongside Clint.

"Whataya think of the Outback?" he asked.

"Except for those," Clint said, pointing to the animals in the distance, "I could be home."

"I ain't never been to America," Matthew said. "What would you see instead of kangaroos and dingos?"

"Wild horses, wolves, cougars—"

"Big cats," Matthew said. "We ain't got those, but our dingos are kinda dangerous."

"That's what Meg said."

"She tell you she was carried off by one when she was small?" Matthew asked.

"Not a word," Clint said. "Does she remember?"

"Beats me," Matthew said. "You'd have to ask her. My dad and hers ran after it and got her back with no harm done but a few teeth marks."

Clint remembered seeing what looked like bite marks on Meg's fine butt.

"I'll ask her," he said.

Chapter Thirty

When they came within sight of a sprawling ranch, Clint was surprised. He expected to find much less. There was a large, rambling one-level house, a large barn and a corral that held about a dozen good-looking horses. Whoever had been looking over the property had taken damned good care of it.

Katy pulled the buckboard to a stop in front of the house, which had a large porch. She and Meg dropped down as the three male cousins dismounted, along with Clint.

"I guess you'll be in the bunkhouse with the boys," Matthew said to Clint.

"That's fine," Clint said. "How many hands do you have?"

"No, I mean James and Daniel," Matthew said. "It's just us. Katy and I stay in the house."

"No problem," Clint said.

"We can move your bag over there."

"I don't have much," Clint assured him. "Just worry about making Meg comfortable."

"No problem," Matthew said. "We got her room ready."

They mounted the porch to follow Katy and Meg into the house, but Matthew turned.

"Me and the boys handle the horses, and Katy looks after the house and does the cookin'."

"I might as well ask this now," Clint said, "and get it out of the way."

Matthew looked at Clint, and then at the gun on his hip.

"What's that?"

"There's no resentment for your father leaving this place to Meg?"

"None."

"Why not?"

"Because it was always hers," Matthew said. "I mean, her father's. My father was looking after it after Uncle Danny died, and always figured Meg would come back for it." He slapped Clint on the back. "Come on, let's go inside and have a cold drink."

Clint didn't know what Matthew meant by a drink, but it turned out to be lemonade. After the hot ride from the train station, that suited him just fine.

The inside of the house was as expensive as the outside. If it was all Katy's work, Clint was impressed.

They gathered in a spacious room, which had a large window that overlooked the front. He could see the barn and corral from there.

Katy came in with glasses of ice cold lemonade on a tray. They all took a glass, and Katy raised hers.

"Welcome home, Cousin Meg," she announced, and they all drank.

"I have to admit," Meg said, "I never expected this kind of reception."

"What did you expect?" Matthew asked. "This is your home. It always has been."

"But I've been gone so long."

"Don't matter," James said.

"Your room is still here," Matthew said.

"Come on," Katy said, putting her hand out, "I kept it clean for ya."

Meg looked at Clint, then took Katy's hand and followed her.

Daniel looked at Clint.

"Where's your bag?" he asked. "I'll put it in the bunkhouse for ya."

"I don't have enough stuff for my own bag," Clint said. "It's in Meg's trunk. I'll get it later."

"You always wear that gun?" James asked. He was the youngest, and wide-eyed as he asked the question.

"Always," Clint said.

"Are you good with it?"

"Yes."

"No rifle?" Daniel asked.

"I didn't bring it," Clint said. "I travelled light. I'll tell you what I would like, though."

"A real drink?" Daniel asked, his eyes lighting up. "We got that in the bunkhouse, too."

"And a look at the stock in that corral," Clint added.

"You boys show him the stock," Matthew said, "and get him that drink."

"This way, Clint!" James said.

Daniel and James led Clint out of the house and over to the corral. The bunkhouse was off to one side, where Clint had not seen it.

Clint stopped at the corral to look over the Australian horses.

"These are good-looking animals," he said.

"They'll be better when they're broke," Daniel said.

"Who breaks them?" Clint asked.

"We all do," James said, "except Katy, of course."

"You break much wild stock in the West, Clint?" Daniel asked.

"When I was younger," Clint admitted. "These days, not so much."

Chapter Thirty-One

Katy cooked dinner and they all sat at the long wooden table in the house.

"This is mighty good chicken, Katy," Clint said, as they ate.

"That's Aussie game fowl," Daniel said. "Those birds are good for fightin' and eatin'."

"It's cruel to make them fight," Katy said.

"Crueler than killin' 'em and eatin' 'em?" James asked, laughing.

"At least this way they get put to good use," Katy said, setting down another plate of vegetables, and then returning to the kitchen.

"Why doesn't Katy sit and eat?" Clint asked.

"She always feeds us first," Daniel said. "That's what our mother used to do."

"Well, I think she deserves to sit and eat some of this, herself."

"Why don't you go and tell 'er that, Clint?" Meg asked, with a smile.

"I think I will." He wiped his mouth, set his napkin down, got up and walked to the kitchen. When he walked in Katy turned quickly, holding a ladle like a weapon.

"Oh, it's you, Mr. Adams," the pretty young girl said. "I thought it was going be one of my brothers, come to argue about fighting Aussies."

"Not at all," Clint said. "I was going to make an argument for you to come sit down and eat with us. This is a fine meal, and you should be enjoying it."

"My momma never ate til all the men did," she said.

"That was a while ago, Katy," Clint said. "I'm a guest, and I'd like you to come and eat with us."

She thought a moment, then said, "All right, then." She set the ladle down and followed Clint from the kitchen.

"Come and sit, Katy!" Meg called. "Right here." She patted the bench next to her and filled a plate for her cousin.

Clint went back to his seat across from the two girls and continued eating.

"If no one minds, I have a few questions," Clint said, as the meal came to a close.

"Go ahead," Matthew said, "We ain't hidin' anythin.'"

"Before we left Sydney a lawyer named Carstairs tried to cheat Meg out of this property," Clint explained. "Do any of you know why he'd do that?"

"Maybe," Matthew said, "because he's a lawyer."

"It comes natural to those fellers," James commented.

"That could be one reason," Clint said. "From what I can see, this home you've built here is worth more than he offered, but is there anything I don't know about?"

"Like what?" Daniel asked.

"Well, I see you've got some fine horses," Clint said. "What else might there be to interest a man like Carstairs. The only reason I can think of for him to buy something cheap would be to sell it at a higher price."

"That makes sense," Matthew said.

"So what's here that makes it worth his while and money?" Clint asked.

Matthew wiped his mouth and dropped his napkin on the table.

"If you don't mind, Mr. Adams," he said, "I don't know you any better than I know this Carstairs. I don't feel quite right talkin' to you about our family holdin's."

He walked away from the table. His two brothers took his cue and followed.

"I'm sorry about them, Clint," Katy said.

"I'll talk to them, Clint" Meg said, "and see what I can find out." She looked at Katy. "Come on, girl, I'll help you clean up."

As Katy started picking up plates Clint sidled up to Meg and said, "See what you can find out from Katy. How'd they know we'd be on that train, today?"

Meg nodded and carried some plates into the kitchen while Clint went into the front room.

"Katy," Meg said, setting the plates down, "what's goin' on?"

"Whataya mean, Meg?"

"How did you know when I was comin' in?"

"We been meeting the train every day, figurin' you'd be on it, eventually."

"And what is it the boys don't want to talk to Clint about?" Meg asked.

"They just don't know 'im, Meg."

"And what about me? They don't know me, either."

"Aw Meg, you been away a long time," Katy said, "but you're still family."

"So do you think Matthew would talk to me?"

"All you gotta do is ask 'im."

"And do you know what's goin' on?"

Katy said, "The boys don't talk to me about much, Meg. I'm young, and I'm a girl."

"Well, let's see if they'll talk to me."

Chapter Thirty-Two

Clint left the house and walked to the corral to look the horses over again.

"What do you see?" Meg asked, coming up behind him.

"Good stock," Clint said.

"Good enough for Carstairs to want?" she asked, standing next to him.

"No."

"Well then," she said, "I guess I should go and talk to Matthew."

"I'll tell you what," Clint said, "tomorrow morning let's you and me go for a ride."

"Where?"

He waved his arm and said, "Out there."

"What do you think we'll find?"

"I don't know," Clint said, "but I'd like to take a look."

"All right," she said. "Let's go back to the house and I'll get your bedroll and clothes out of my trunk."

"Good idea."

Clint waited in the front room while Meg went to unpack.

Katy came in, arms folded across her chest, and stared at him.

"So what's goin' on between you and cousin Meg?" she asked.

"We're friends," he said. "I came with her because I thought she might need help."

She looked at his hip.

"And that gun," she said, "do you wear it all the time?"

"I do, yes."

"Why?"

"People have a habit of trying to kill me," he said. "I like stopping them."

"So what do they call you in America?" she asked. "A gunfighter?"

"Some people call me that."

"What do you call yourself?"

"Just a fella who likes to stay alive."

Meg came into the room carrying Clint's bedroll and a bag with his new clothes in it.

"I unpacked my bags and filled one for you," she said, handing it to him.

"You two ain't stayin' in the same room?" Katy asked.

"I don't think that'd be a good idea, do you?" Clint asked.

Katy shrugged, turned and left the room.

"Those boys seem to treat her like a maid," Clint said.

"That's the way they were brought up," Meg said. "Those are their ways."

"It's not your way."

"Remember," she said, "I've been away in America a long time."

"Well," he said, "I guess I'll go and get settled in the bunkhouse."

"Come and have a cup of coffee with me on the porch before you turn in."

"I'll do that."

Clint slung the bedroll over his shoulder and carried the bag out of the house. He walked to the bunkhouse and entered, there was no touch of Katy, there, just a place where men slept and played cards. At that moment James and Daniel were sitting at a table, drinking whiskey.

"Thought you'd be here soon enough," James said. "Whiskey?"

"Don't mind if I do."

James poured a glass and handed it to him. He sat at the table with them.

"You fellas willing to talk?" he asked.

"Matthew says we ain't to say a word to you, Mr. Adams," James said.

"You boys do everything Matthew tells you to do?" Clint asked.

"He's been in charge since Pa died," Daniel said.

"We ain't ones to cross 'im," James added.

Clint sipped his whiskey.

"Okay, then," he said. "I won't make it any harder on you by asking any more questions."

"We appreciate that," James said. "You can have any bunk against that wall, Clint. Me and Matthew are on this side."

"Thanks." He set the glass down and carried his gear to a bunk. "You boys don't mind sleeping out here instead of in the house?"

"Nah," Daniel said, "we like it better out here."

"We ain't got Katy tellin' us to take off our boots, or wash up," James said. "She's worse than Ma was."

"Doesn't she mind being treated like a maid?"

"Whataya mean?" Daniel asked, frowning.

"She's just doin' what Ma used to do," James said, also confused.

"But she's not your Ma," Clint said. "She's a young woman. Doesn't she want to go to parties, or dances?"

"Out here?" Daniel asked. "Ain't no such things."

" 'sides," James said, "we don't just treat her like Ma. She can ride and shoot."

"Katy's a McGregor, through-and-through," Daniel said.

Clint opened the bag and took out his clothes.

"I guess that's good, then," he said.

Chapter Thirty-Three

"You play poker?" Daniel asked Clint.

"Some."

"Wanna play with us?" James asked.

"Sure." Clint turned from his bunk. "What stakes?"

"Aw shucks" James said, "we play for match sticks."

"I don't think I have any," Clint said.

"No problem," Daniel said. "We got plenty."

Daniel walked to a sideboard and came back with a box filled with matchsticks.

"Take a handful and let's play."

***

The McGregor boys played poker to pass the time. They were both terrible at it, so Clint took it easy on them. Still, most of the sticks went his way.

"You've probably played for higher stakes than this," James said.

"Some," Clint agreed,

"And against famous gamblers?" Daniel asked.

"Some," Clint said, again.

"Like who?" James asked. "You know, we've read some books about the American West."

"Have you, now?"

"Yeah," James said, "I got 'em in my bunk. Did you ever play with Bat Masterson?"

"I did."

"And Wyatt Earp? Doc Holliday?"

"All of them," Clint said. "They're all friends of mine."

"Really?" James asked. "What are they like?"

"Just like regular folks," Clint said, "trying to live their lives the best way they can."

James wanted to ask more questions, but at that moment Matthew came in.

"Poker for sticks again?" he demanded. "I tol' you—"

"We just thought Clint'd like to play, Matt," Daniel said, "that's all."

"You boys have work to do before sundown," Matthew said. "Get to it!"

"Sure, Matt, sure," Daniel said.

He and James dropped their cards and left their sticks on the table as they rushed out.

"You rule with an iron hand, don't you, Matthew?" Clint asked.

"Somebody's got to," Matthew said. "They're good boys, but they're as dumb as those match sticks."

Matthew walked to the table, swept the matches into the box, then poured himself a drink.

"What're you really doin' here, Clint?" he asked.

"I'm just trying to help Meg," Clint said.

"Meg's got her family to help her," Matthew said. "We don't need you."

"Well," Clint said, "if you don't mind, I'll wait for Meg to tell me that."

"She tells me you're goin' ridin' together tomorrow," Matthew said.

"That's right."

"What for?"

"Just to take a good look at her holdings."

"I hope you ain't thinkin' she's gonna marry you," Matthew said.

"Good God," Clint said, "I hope she isn't thinking that, either."

Matthew smiled, shook his head and left.

Clint walked to his bunk and finished unpacking. He figured he would be there a while longer.

***

As the sun started to go down Clint left the bunkhouse and walked back to the house. Meg was sitting on the porch with a pot of coffee and two cups. Clint sat in a chair so that the table with the coffee was between them. Meg poured a cup for him. He sipped it.

"Wow, that's good," he said.

"I told Katy you like it strong."

Clint drank some more before setting the cup down.

"I've got to tell you, I don't like the way your family treats that girl," he told Meg.

"Well, you've already made a change by getting her to eat with us."

"Why would they let you eat with them if they don't let her?" Clint asked. "You're both girls."

"Yes, but I'm the girl who owns the place."

"Meg," Clint said, "you really didn't know that all these cousins would be here?"

"I figured after Uncle Frank died his boys would go off with the four winds," she said. "I didn't even think about Katy. She was such a little thing when I left."

"But they all stayed."

"Yes, they did," Meg said.

"So what are you going to do now?"

"Like you said," Meg replied, "we'll ride out tomorrow and take a look at my holdings before I decide that."

"Okay," Clint said, picking up the coffee cup "One step at a time."

Chapter Thirty-Four

Clint slept as well as he could in the bunkhouse with both Daniel and James snoring their heads off. Meg had told him to make sure he came to the house the next morning for breakfast, so he finally gave up trying to sleep, got dressed and went to the house. It was early, so he sat in a chair on the porch and began to doze until Katy found him there.

"Did you sleep out here all night?" Katy asked. "What did those boys do to you?"

"I've only been here about an hour," Clint said. "Those two boys, though, they sure snore alike."

"Well, Meg and I are starting breakfast," Katy said. "You stay here and I'll bring out a cup of coffee."

"Thank you."

She went inside and came right back with a coffee mug.

"There you go," she said. "I'll come out and get you when breakfast's ready."

"Thank you, Katy."

Clint sat there, staring out at the corral, sipping the coffee slowly. It was strong and he was enjoying it. He was almost to the bottom of the mug when Daniel and James came over from the bunkhouse.

"You got up early," Daniel said. "I hope me and James' snoring didn't wake ya."

"Actually, I didn't get much sleep," Clint said, "but I expect I'll get used to it."

They stepped up onto the porch and James asked, "Breakfast ready?"

"Katy said she'd come out and get me when it was," Clint said.

At that moment the door opened and Katy stuck her head out.

"Breakfast is served, boys."

"Yee-haw, let's eat," James said. He pushed past her into the house, with Daniel right behind him.

Katy held the door open for Clint, but he reversed the gesture and said, "After you."

"Thank you, Sir."

He followed her to the table, which was covered with plates of flapjacks, eggs and several kinds of meat. There were also a couple of baskets of biscuits.

"Sit and eat!" Meg said, as she seated herself. "Sit next to me, Katy."

They all sat down, with Clint across from the two girls, and Matthew at the head of the table.

"Did you sleep all right in the bunkhouse, Mr. Adams?" Matthew asked.

"I'm afraid our snorin' kept him awake, Matt," James said, laughing.

"I told the boys I'll get used to it," Clint said.

"That's silly," Katy said. "If he can't get any sleep in the bunkhouse, Clint should move into the main house. We got room."

"The bunkhouse is fine, Katy," Clint assured her, "but thank you. Let's all just eat."

They all started filling their plates and eating.

"Cousin, Meg," Matthew asked, "you and Clint still goin' ridin' today?"

"Yes, we are, Matthew," Meg said. "I've been away so long I want to look the property over."

"Then maybe one of us should go with you to make sure you don't get lost."

"I think we'll be fine," Clint said. "You boys all have work to do."

"I was thinkin' of Katy goin' with you," Matthew said. "What about it, Katy?"

"I'd love it!" Katy squealed, then looked at Meg. "Is it all right with you?"

"It's fine with me if it's fine with Clint," Meg said.

"I don't have a problem with it," Clint said.

"The boys'll saddle some horses for you after breakfast," Matthew said.

"And I'll pack some food for us," Katy added. "We might be out there a while, dependin' on how much you wanna see."

"This is a fine breakfast, Katy," Clint said, putting another slab of meat on his plate, "a fine meal."

"Thank you, Clint."

"Yeah," Matthew said, "our Katy's a fine cook. Not as good as Mama was, but very fine."

James and Daniel went for the same biscuit, and wrestled over it until it broke in half.

"Settle down, boys," Matthew said. "There's plenty."

***

Matthew sent Daniel and James out to the barn to saddle the horses, even though they wanted to eat more.

"You had enough," Matthew said. "Go on!"

They each grabbed another biscuit before leaving the table.

"I'll help you clean up, Katy," Meg said.

When Meg and Katy were in the kitchen, Clint and Matthew each had another cup of coffee.

"What do you think you and Meg are going to find out there, Mr. Adams?" Matthew asked.

"Well," Clint said, "that remains to be seen, Matthew. I'm just thinking there's something more here than those horses and this house that Carstairs is trying to get."

"Then maybe you shoulda asked him, before you left Sydney."

"You know what?" Clint asked. "I think you're right."

Chapter Thirty-Five

Clint, Meg and Katy walked over to the barn, where Daniel and James were waiting with three saddled horses. All three were brown, standing about 16 hands. Their necks were arched, and their heads well-set.

"These are Australian Stock Horses," Daniel said, handing Clint the reins of one of them. "They're sturdy and got lots of endurance. You can push 'em as hard as you want."

Meg took the reins from James.

"This one's mine," Katy said, of the third. "I raised him."

All three of them mounted up. The horse felt good underneath Clint.

"Thanks, boys," he said. "See you for supper."

As they rode away Clint heard James yell, "Katy's with you, who's gonna cook supper?"

***

Clint decided not to push the horses at all. There was no hurry. So they rode at an easy pace, just looking the terrain over.

Katy showed them wide expanses of flats, some mountain ranges, lakes, flora that was mostly Eucalyptus trees. They encountered kangaroos, dingos—luckily, in the distance—and in a couple of lakes, Alligators.

When they stopped once to fill their canteens Clint thought he saw some people in the distance.

"What do you see?" Meg asked.

"I don't know," Clint said. "I just thought I saw—"

Before he could finish, they were suddenly surrounded by a band of people he assumed were a tribe of Aborigines, many carrying spears. There were about a dozen, and Clint didn't like how easily they had come up on him. Then again, this was their land.

He put his hand on his gun, and Katy grabbed his arm.

"No, don't!" she shouted. "These are my friends."

"Friends?"

She walked over to one of them, who appeared to be the leader.

"This is Jay-Jay," she said. "He was friends with my father."

"Who these people?" Jay-Jay asked in broken English.

"This is Meg," Katy said, touching Meg's arm, "she is family, a cousin." She put her hand on Clint's arm. "This is Clint. He is a friend."

"He has weapon," Jay-Jay said.

"He won't use it," Meg said. "It's for self-defense."

Jay-Jay stared at Clint and his gun, then beckoned Katy aside. They spoke so that Clint and Meg couldn't hear.

When they were done Katy came over to Clint, while Jay-Jay stood aside with his people. They were all male, of different sizes and shapes, all wearing some sort of loin cloths.

"What's going on, Katy?"

"They want to see Clint shoot," Katy said. "They're curious."

"I don't like doing trick shooting if I don't have to," Clint said, "but I could make this an exception."

Katy looked at the rocks and trees around them.

"What should you shoot at?" she asked.

"Tell him to have his people hold their spears straight up.

Katy went back to Jay-Jay to relay the message. Before long all twelve of them were holding their spears with the points aimed at the sky.

"Is that good?" Katy asked.

"It's fine."

Clint drew swiftly, and fired six times. The points of six spears flew into the air. He quickly reloaded and holstered the gun.

"Oh my God!" Katy said.

The Aborigines were shocked, and impressed. Six of them still had their spears. The other six didn't seem upset that their spears had been rendered useless.

Katy went back to Jay-Jay, spoke with him, and then the Aborigines walked off and disappeared into the Outback.

"He wanted us to come to his village, but I told him it would have to be another time," Katy said, as she walked back.

"That's probably just as well."

"That was amazing, Clint," Katy said. "Are you—I mean, in America, are you famous?"

"He is," Meg said. "They call him the Gunsmith."

"I knew it!" Katy said. "I had a feeling you were special."

"We're all special in some way, Katy," he said. "Where to next?"

"What else do you want to see?"

They had already stopped at a couple of lakes and water holes, where Clint had let the water run through his fingers. There was no sign of gold or anything else.

"That mountain," he said. "How far is it?"

"That's a day's ride, Clint."

That was what he had figured.

"Maybe another time, then," he said. "How much of this land is yours?"

"To tell you the truth, I don't really know," she said, "and I don't think my father knew. He just always said that all we could see was ours. And now it's Meg's."

"Let's ride a little more before we head back," he suggested, and they mounted up.

Chapter Thirty-Six

When the first shot came, Clint reacted immediately. The women just swiveled their heads around in shock, unsure of what was happening.

"Get off those horses!" Clint shouted.

By the time the second shot came, they had all dismounted and their horses had run off. They took cover in a dry riverbed.

"Keep your heads down," Clint ordered. He stuck his head up, trying to see where the shots had come from. There were some hills in the distance, which were the most likely place.

When he ducked back down, he looked at Meg and Katy.

"Who's shooting at us?" Katy asked. "And why?"

"If we were in America, I'd assume they were shooting at me because of who I am."

"Does that happen?" she asked.

"All the time," he said. "But here, I just don't know."

"Do you think they were shooting at me?" Meg asked.

"Why you?" Katy asked, turning her head.

"Because I'm the new owner."

"That makes sense," Clint said. "Carstairs may have sent somebody here with a rifle."

"The lawyer?" Katy asked. "Why?"

"He wants this property," Meg said. "I guess he figures if he kills me, he can buy it from whichever of you inherits it."

"That'd be Matthew, according to father's will."

Katy looked at Clint.

"Are you going to shoot back?"

"Wherever they are, they're out of range of my gun," Clint said. "I'd need a rifle."

"Then what do we do?" Meg asked. "We're pinned down and our horses are gone."

"First we have to find out if they're still out there waiting to take another shot," Clint said.

"How do we do that?" Katy asked.

"You two just stay down," Clint said.

He stood up, hoping if there was a third shot, he would be able to locate the source. But it appeared whoever it was had taken two shots and withdrew. No doubt they would be trying again another time.

"Looks like they lit out," Clint said. "You can stand."

Meg and Katy stood up, and the three of them stepped from the dry bed.

"Now what?" Meg asked.

"We have to find our horses," Clint said. "I want to locate the spot they took the shots from."

If we can't find the horses we'll have to walk back," Meg said.

"We could probably get Jay-Jay and his people to help," Katy said, "but I don't think we'll have to do that."

"Why not?" Meg asked.

"I told you, I raised my horse from a colt," Katy said. "He won't have gone far."

She turned and shouted, "Baby? Come on, Baby. Come here!"

From the distance they heard the sound of horse's hooves, and then Baby appeared. The horse ran right up to Katy, who grabbed him around the neck.

"That's a good Baby," she said, stroking him. "I'll take Baby and go find your horses," she told Clint and Meg.

"All right," Clint said. "We'll wait here. They may drift back now that the shooting has stopped."

Katy mounted up and rode off. Clint and Meg looked around and found a rock to sit on.

"Well, I'm really glad I brought you with me now," Meg said. "I doubt they were shooting at you, Clint. That means somebody would rather kill me than have me inherit."

"That means Carstairs, or one of your male cousins."

"Oh no," she said, "it can't be Matthew, Daniel or James."

"If it was Carstairs, he must've sent a telegram to Parramatta Junction."

"But to who?"

"I'll have to go there to find out," Clint said, "but I think you should be prepared for the worst, Meg."

"You mean, one of my cousins?"

Clint nodded.

"I can't believe that," she said.

Before long they heard horses approaching, and then Katy appeared, leading their two mounts.

"Luckily, they didn't go far," she said.

They all took drinks from their canteens, and then mounted up.

"The shots came from over there," Clint said, pointing, and off they rode.

***

When they reached the hills, it took a while to locate the spot.

"They were here," Clint said, dismounting.

"How can you tell?" Katy asked.

"Tracks," Clint said, pointing at the ground. Then he reached down and picked something up. "And one of them left a spent shell casing. I don't recognize it."

"Let me see," Katy said.

Clint handed it to her.

"It's British," she said, "a Martin-Henry rifle. She handed it back and Clint put it in his pocket.

"Are we going to Parramatta Junction now?" Meg asked.

"No, it's too late. The boys are probably wondering where we are now," Clint said, thinking that one of them might already know. "I'll ride over there tomorrow."

"And I'll stay home?" Meg asked.

"No," Clint said, "I think you'll be safer with me."

"She'll be safe at home with us," Katy pointed out.

"I'd rather have her by my side where I can watch her, Katy," Clint said. He hoped the girl wouldn't take offense.

"Well, all right," Katy said. "As long as she's safe. I still can't believe someone tried to kill her."

"The proof's right here," Clint said, patting his pocket. "Come on, let's get back."

"The boys are probably starving," Katy said. "None of them would ever think about starting supper."

As they went to their horses Clint pulled Meg to one side.

"We don't want Katy realizing I suspect one of her brothers," he whispered.

"I still can't believe that," Meg said. "They all seemed so happy to see me."

"Remember, Meg," Clint said, "you don't know them that well."

"Still . . ." she said, and they mounted up.

Chapter Thirty-Seven

When they rode up to the house the three McGregor boys were on the porch.

"Where've you been?" James asked. I'm starving."

They dismounted and Katy said, "I'll start supper."

"You boys take care of the horses," Matthew said.

James and Daniel took the reins and walked the horses to the barn.

"We were wonderin' what was takin' you so long?" Matthew asked.

"Somebody shot at us," Meg said.

"What?" He looked at Meg. "Are you all right?"

"Yes," she said, "they missed and then ran off."

"Who was it?" Matthew asked. "Did you see?"

"No," Meg said, "but Clint found something." She opened the front door. "I'm going to help Katy."

Clint took the shell from his pocket and handed it to Matthew.

"This is from a Martin-Henry," Matthew said.

"That's what Katy said," Clint told him.

"She's a smart girl," Matthew said.

"Do you know anybody around here who has a Martin-Henry rifle?" Clint asked.

"Well, I know we don't," Matthew said, handing the shell back.

"What about the bush rangers I've been hearing about?" Clint asked.

"We haven't had any trouble with bush rangers in a long time," Matthew said. "Not since they hung Ned Kelly."

"Are there any other ranches nearby?" Clint asked.

"No," Matthew said, "but you can find one a day's ride in either direction, east or west."

"And do you know your neighbors?"

"We don't get to see our neighbors very often," Matthew said, "but every now and then we'll run into someone in Parramatta Junction when we're picking up supplies."

"Who are they?"

"Well, to the west is a family named Gibson, a couple of boys and a girl. Their father was friends with ours for a while, but since they're both dead we don't see much of each other."

"And to the east?"

"Ben Wheeler."

"Really," Clint said. "Ben?"

"Do you know him?"

"We met on the ship on the way over," Clint said, "and he recommend a lawyer for Meg, to help her get away from Carstairs."

"He's very rich," Matthew said, "and well known."

"I'm finding that out," Clint said.

"I don't see where either one of them would have reason to try and shoot Meg," Matthew said.

"Maybe not," Clint said, "but I could always ask them."

"If you want to visit them, I could ride around with you."

"Meg and I are going to the Junction tomorrow," Clint said. "I want to see if the lawyer, Carstairs, sent a telegram to anyone."

"You think he sent a telegram to someone telling them to murder Meg?" Matthew asked. "But that would point a finger right at him."

"The word murder doesn't have to appear in the telegram," Clint said. "Or he might even have had someone else send it, like an assistant."

"Well," Matthew said, "when you decide to see the Gibsons or Wheeler, let me know."

James and Daniel came running back from the barn.

"Supper ready yet?" James asked.

"They just started preparing it," Matthew said. "Clint just told me someone took a couple of shots at him and

Meg with a Martin-Henry rifle. You boys know anybody who has one?"

"Not me," James said.

"Me neither," Daniel added.

"Let's go inside and see how far along they are."

The two younger boys rushed into the house, with Matthew right behind them, shaking his head.

Clint touched the spent shell in his shirt, realizing he had never told Matthew there had been two shots.

Chapter Thirty-Eight

At super Daniel and James dug voraciously into their meat pies while Katy and Meg talked about the shooting. Then Katy looked at Clint and asked, "Can I tell them?"

"Tell us what?" James asked.

Katy waited to hear what Clint had to say.

"I suppose so."

"Clint is a famous gunfighter of the American West called The Gunsmith."

"What?" James said, almost choking. "I have a book about you."

"Yes," Clint said, "there are one or two."

"And you should see him shoot," Katy said. "We ran into Jay-Jay and his people and Clint gave a demonstration."

"Aw, I wish I coulda seen that," James said. "Clint, could you show us?"

"Before Clint could answer, Matthew turned on Katy and said, angrily, "I thought I told you to stay away from those savages."

"Jay-Jay and his people are not savages," Katy argued.

"Are they runnin' around out there in bare feet and loin cloths?"

"Well—"

"They're savages!"

Katy put her head down and continued to eat.

Matthew looked at Meg.

"Is this true? You brought a gunfighter here with you?" he demanded.

"I brought a friend," she said.

"And now somebody's taken a shot at him, putting you and Katy in danger."

"I doubt they were shooting at him," Meg said. "Nobody in this country knows who he is, or even that he's here."

"Carstairs knows he's here," Matthew pointed out. "He might even know his reputation."

"I still think the shots was meant for me," Meg said, "and I'm sorry Katy was put in danger."

"It wasn't your fault, Meg," Katy assured her.

"Still," Meg said, "I'd never forgive myself if anything happened to you."

Katy leaned over and hugged Meg.

"Come on," Meg said to Katy, "let's clean up." She said to the men, "We'll bring coffee out to the porch."

"Great!" James said, as he and Daniel got to their feet. "Maybe Clint'll shoot for us!"

"James—" Matthew started.

"Never mind, Matthew," Clint said. "There's no harm in it."

The four men went out to the porch to wait for coffee. Clint was still eyeing Matthew as the possible shooter. Maybe a demonstration would change his mind about trying again.

"Whataya wanna shoot?" James asked. "Empty bottles? Playing cards?"

"Bottles sound good."

"There's some out back." James ran around the house and came back with an armful of bottles of varying sizes. Then he stood on the porch and set them down.

"How'ya wanna do this?"

"I don't know," Clint said. "Just toss them, I guess."

"I'll toss one," James said, picking one up. "Ready?"

"Ready."

He tossed it high into the air. Clint drew and fired, shattering it into little pieces.

"Wow!" James said. He turned to Daniel while Clint holstered his gun. "C'mon Daniel, toss one with me."

"Okay."

They each picked one up and looked at Clint.

"Ready," Clint said.

Each man tossed a bottle into the air. Clint drew and fired twice, shattering both, even though they were far apart.

Clint was sure the girls could hear the shots inside. . .

***

Katy looked at Meg as the sound of the shots came to them.

"Meg," she asked, "do you think one of my brothers shot at you and Clint?"

"I hope not, Katy," Meg said.

"But that's what Clint thinks, isn't it?"

"Clint doesn't know the boys," Meg said. "My bet is on the lawyer hiring somebody to do it."

"But who?"

"I don't know," Meg said. "Maybe he hired 'em and sent 'em here to do it."

"If he did that there'd be no telegram for you to find tomorrow," Katy said.

"That's right."

"What'll Clint do then?"

"I don't know, Katy," Meg said, "but this is the reason I brought him here. To help me. I just didn't know all my cousins would be here."

"If my dad hadn't stuck to your dad's wishes, this wouldn't be happening. He woulda left the property to the boys."

"Or to the oldest boy," Meg said.

"Matthew."

Meg nodded.

"Matthew wouldn't shoot at you, Meg."

"I hope you're right, Katy."

Chapter Thirty-Nine

The girls came out to the porch with a pot of coffee and a bunch of clean cups.

"That's it for the shooting," Meg said. "Coffee's served."

Katy set the pot down on the table, put her hands on her hips and stared out.

"Who's gonna clean up all that broken glass?" she demanded. Then she turned and glared at Daniel and James. "You get it all swept up and then you can have some coffee."

"Yeah, all right," James muttered. "I'll fetch a broom and a shovel."

When he came back Clint and Matthew were seated, drinking coffee. Meg and Katy had pulled over two more chairs and joined them.

"Here," James said, putting the shovel in Daniel's hands. Both boys went and started picking up shards of broken glass.

"Were the boys impressed?" Katy asked.

"We were real impressed," Daniel said. "Clint don't miss."

"Ain't it amazin'?" Katy asked.

"I'm thinkin' whoever shot at you today better be real careful from here on in," Daniel said.

"I think I better have a rifle with me when we ride out again," Clint commented.

"We got rifles," Matthew said. "I'll get you one tomorrow."

"Thanks."

"The Junction is a pretty long ride," Matthew said. "It could happen again anywhere between here and there."

"I know it."

"But you want them to try again, don't you?" Matthew said. "So you can get 'em next time."

"They'll only get one more chance at me, yes," Clint said.

"But, if there's two of 'em—" Katy said.

"There was two shots," Clint said, "but that doesn't mean there were two shooters."

"Well," Matthew said, "if this lawyer, Carstairs, knew who you was, and your reputation, he'd probably be smart enough to send two shooters."

"One or two, doesn't make a difference to me," Clint said.

"You got a lot of confidence," Matthew said.

"It's kept me alive this long."

"Let's hope it keeps you alive longer," Matthew said.

***

Alan Carstairs was eating supper in his favorite Sydney restaurant when Edward Hopkins walked in and joined him.

"You want something to eat?" Carstairs asked.

"I already ate."

"Then have a drink."

There was a bottle of whiskey and two glasses on the table. Hopkins poured himself a shot and downed it.

"What's on your mind?" Carstairs asked.

"No word from the Junction yet."

"It would take them a while to get there after they kill Adams," Carstairs told him. "We'll have to be patient."

"I keep checkin' the telegraph office."

"Well, stop," Carstairs said. "When the telegram comes they'll bring it to me. Just stay in your hotel and wait."

"Yeah, all right," Hopkins said, standing.

"Hold on."

Hopkins paused.

"What about Kingman?"

"Oh," Hopkins said, "he's dead."

"That's good. Okay, go ahead. And relax. This will all come out the way it's supposed to."

"I hope you're right."

Hopkins left and Carstairs went back to his meal. He had plans for the night. His Aborigine whore was waiting for him.

***

Daniel and James finished their coffee and went off to get some work done before dark. Katy and Meg took the pot and cups back into the house. That left Clint alone on the porch with Matthew.

"You see my sister with that savage, Jay-Jay?"

"I did," Clint said. "They seemed like friends."

"You can't make friends with those people," Matthew said. "My father tried."

"Maybe he wasn't as likeable as Katy."

"My little sister's a foolish girl," Matthew said. "Look how impressed she and my brothers are with you."

"And you're not?"

"No, I'm not," Matthews said. "I'm thirty-four years old and I've seen some. They ain't seen nothin'."

"So you're going to set them straight, huh?"

"You bet," Matthew said.

"You think this property should've been yours, don't you, Matthew?"

Matthew stood up.

"Just keep watchin' your step, Adams," he said, and walked away.

Meg came out, saw her cousin storming away.

"What was that about?" she asked.

"He wants me to keep watching my back."

Meg looked hard at Clint.

"He didn't admit it was him, did he?"

"No."

"That's good."

"I know you don't want it to be him, Meg, but—"

"I don't want it to be him for Katy's sake," Meg said.

"Well," Clint said, "if it wasn't him, it's going to take us a hell of a lot longer to find out who it was."

"Clint," Meg said, "if he wants this property bad enough, I'd rather give it to him then . . ."

". . . then fight your cousin?"

Meg nodded.

"Then offer it to him, Meg," Clint said, "and see what he says."

"And if it was him, will you let him go?"

Clint stood up.

"I'm not in the habit of forgiving people who try to kill me," he said, and walked away.

Chapter Forty

When Clint entered the bunkhouse that night, James and Daniel were sitting there at the table with cards and matchsticks.

"A few hands before you turn in?" Daniel asked.

"Why not?" Clint asked.

He sat across from them as James started dealing.

"You never take that gun off, do ya?" James asked.

"When I'm in bed," Clint said, "but it's always within reach."

"Must be a hard way to live," Daniel said.

"Maybe," Clint said, picking up his cards, "but it keeps me from dying."

They played a few hands before Clint figured the two brothers were relaxed enough to answer questions.

"So what were you boys doing while the ladies and I were out riding?"

"We had work to do," Daniel said.

"Yeah," James said, "Matthew kept us busy while he was out riding."

"Oh? Where did he go?"

"He was checking our wild stock," James said, "said he thought a couple had got out of the corral."

"And did he find them?" Clint asked.

"Nope," Daniel said, "came back empty handed. Counted the horses in the corral and realized he was wrong."

"Oh?" Clint said. "Does he often admit when he's wrong?"

They both laughed and James said, "Never!"

They played a few more hands before the three of them turned in. Before long, James and Daniel were snoring away. Clint got up from his bunk and walked outside with his gunbelt over his shoulder.

He stood just outside the door and thought about what James and Daniel had told him. After he, Meg and Katy had ridden off, Matthew had also ridden out, supposedly looking for missing stock. Only there was no missing stock. He hadn't asked them if Matthew had a rifle with him. That would have tipped them off that he suspected the shooter had been Matthew.

Clint looked across the compound and thought he saw someone on the porch. He walked across and saw that it was Katy, standing there and just staring off.

"Can't sleep?" he asked, as he approached.

He startled her.

"Oh, Clint!" she said. "No, I-I can't."

"Something on your mind?"

"Bein' shot at, I guess," she said. "It ain't somethin' I'm used to."

"It takes some time."

"Are you used to it?"

"Let's say I expect it," he answered.

"Not even here? So far from home?"

"Well, to tell you the truth," he said "I do suspect they were shooting at Meg. I just happened to be there, like you."

"What do you expect to find tomorrow, at the Junction?"

"Nothing, really."

"Then why go?"

"I figure it's the best way to get them to take another shot," Clint said. "But this time I'll be ready."

"Why not leave Meg here, where it's safe?"

"Do you think she'd stay?"

Katy smiled and said, "No, probably not."

"Besides," Clint added, "that'd just make it easier for the shooter. And one of you might get caught in the crossfire."

"Well," she said, "I hope you get 'em, tomorrow."

"So do I," he said. "Why don't you try to get some sleep now?"

"Those boys still snorin'?" she asked.

He smiled and said, "It's not so bad. Good night.

" 'night, Clint," she said, and went inside.

Chapter Forty-One

When they reached Parramatta Junction they wasted no time finding the telegraph office. The Junction was too small to even be called a town, but apparently it was provided with a telegraph key to keep the Outback connected to Sydney.

Clint and Meg dismounted in front and entered.

"Can I help you folks?" the key operator asked.

"Do you keep a record of telegrams coming in and going out?" Clint asked.

"I certainly do."

"We're looking for one that would have come in from Sydney the past week," Clint said. "Possibly meant for someone at the McGregor ranch."

"And from who in Sydney would it have originated?"

"Possibly a lawyer."

"Allow me to check."

While they waited Meg said, "So nobody tried to shoot us on the way in. Don't you think they would've wanted to do that before we got here?"

"Only if there is a record of such a telegram coming in."

The clerk returned from the backroom.

"No, I'm afraid there's been nothing from Sydney to anyone at the McGregor station."

Clint looked at Meg.

"They call them stations here, not ranches."

"Well," Clint said to the clerk, "have you seen anyone from the McGregor Station around here in the past week?"

"No, Sir."

"Do you know who I'm referring to?"

"I presume either James, Daniel or Matthew McGregor," the clerk said. "I ain't seen none of 'em, lately."

"Is there a general store here?"

"There's Swanson's Trading Post, down the street."

"Thanks."

Outside, Meg asked, "What do you want with the trading post?"

"I want to see if they deal in firearms, specifically that Martin-Henry rifle."

They walked their horses over to the trading post and tied them outside. As they entered Clint could see the post dealt in almost every kind of item you could think of, including liquor at a makeshift bar that seemed to be made of a large wooden door.

"Come on in, folks," a man behind the counter said. He was tall, thin, with wire-framed glasses and sparse hair. "We got everything you could need. Like to start with a drink? You look like you took a long ride to get here." From Swanson's speech pattern and accent, he was decidedly not Australian. His diction was very pronounced, as if he were hiding any kind of accent.

"Have you got cold beer?"

"Indeed I do."

"We'll take two."

"Comin' up," the man said.

He drew two large mugs of beer and set them down on the door.

"Best in Australia," he said.

Clint and Meg sipped it and found it cold and refreshing. They took longer drinks before setting the mugs down.

"Now what else can I do for you?"

"Are you Mr. Swanson?" Clint asked.

"I am, indeed. And what would your name be?"

"I'm Clint Adams and this is Meg McGregor."

"Another McGregor?" the man asked. "Where's young Katy?"

"Back at the station," Meg said.

"She's a sweet little thing. How might you be related?" he asked.

"I'm a cousin," Meg said, "and I happen to own the station, now."

"Is that right?" Swanson said. "Congratulations. You here to stock up?"

"Not quite," she said.

"Mr. Swanson," Clint said, "do you deal in guns?"

"I do, indeed," the man said. "I carry rifles and pistols from all over the world. German, British, American—you, sir, are an American, if I'm not mistaken."

"You're right."

"Then perhaps you can use a Colt, or a Winchester?"

"Actually," Clint said, "I'm interested in a Martin-Henry rifle."

"Ah, an excellent weapon," Swanson said. "Sadly, I no longer have one."

"You had one?"

"And only one," Swanson said. "But I sold it weeks ago."

"Do you remember who you sold it to?"

"I would have to check my records to be certain," Swanson said, "but I believe I sold it to a man named Edward Hopkins."

"Hopkins?"

"I can check."

"Please do."

As Swanson went into the back to look at his records, Meg asked Clint, "Do we know a Hopkins?"

"We do," Clint said. "He owns the hotel Ben Wheeler was staying in."

"Then what was he doing all the way out here?"

"That," Clint said, "is a good question."

Chapter Forty-Two

Swanson came back and said, "Yes, indeed, a Mr. Edward Hopkins."

"Thank you, Mr. Swanson."

Clint and Meg stepped outside.

"Why would this man buy the gun under his real name, and then use it to try and kill me?" she asked.

"He's a hotel owner, not a killer," Clint said.

"Then what did he do with that gun?" she asked.

"He gave it to someone else."

"Who?" she asked. "Oh, you're thinking of Matthew."

"He could have come here to meet with Matthew, make plans, and give him the rifle."

"Then it's Hopkins who's trying to have me killed, not the lawyer?"

"Hopkins is from Sydney," Clint said. "He could've come here representing Carstairs. After all, a lawyer would be smart enough to have others do his dirty work."

"That's true," she said. "So how do we connect this Hopkins to my cousin?"

"Are you ready to believe it might have been Matthew?"

"As you've said, Clint," Meg replied, "I don't know them that well. What do we do?"

"Well, first," Clint said, "I'm going back inside and look at a Winchester."

"I'll wait here."

"No," he said, taking her arm, "you better come in with me. You're too easy a target out here."

They turned and went back inside.

***

When they came out Clint was the proud owner of a brand new Winchester. Well, new to him. It was actually a Winchester 73 Trapper that Clint made sure was in perfect working order.

"Now if he comes for you at a distance," Clint said, "we've got a fighting chance of getting him."

"Do you think you'll be able to see where he's firing from?" she asked.

"I'm going to hear it," Clint said.

"Sounds carry across the Outback," she warned.

"Well, I'll be ready, this time," Clint said. "He's only getting one more chance."

***

The shooter was waiting just outside the Junction, Martin-Henry in hand. This time he wouldn't miss. He would take Meg first, and then put Clint Adams into the ground. The legend of the American West would find the Australian Outback too much for him.

The Martin-Henry was clean, oiled and ready. The shooter had already chosen three or four likely places between the McGregor station and the Junction to make his play.

***

"Is that rifle good enough for the Gunsmith?" Meg asked, as they mounted up.

"This is one of the finest weapons ever made," Clint said. "It'll do the trick."

"The Junction isn't much," Meg said, "but it apparently has everything a man or woman would need. How about a bite before we go back?"

"That sounds good to me."

There was a small Junction Café at the end of the street, just before the train station. They rode over to it, dismounted, tied their horses and went inside to a back table. The place was just about empty.

***

The shooter watched as Clint and Meg went into the café. The place was empty, and even though they were seated at a table in the back, he could have a clear shot through the window. He gave it some thought, but decided he would rather do the deed in the Outback, where nobody would find the bodies.

He waited until they came out before riding ahead of them to one of his chosen spots, where he would wait for his chance.

***

The easy thing to order was a couple of meat pies, and while they were not as tasty as Katy's, they did the trick. They washed them down with a couple of beers, before Meg paid the bill—she was still picking up the tab—and they left.

"All right," Clint said, looking around, "let's mount up and ride out, and give our friend his last chance."

"Are you sure he's going to miss?"

"He took two shots last time," Clint said. "He's going to miss the first one, and then I'll have him."

They rode out.

Chapter Forty-Three

The shooter settled into the first of his chosen spots, but as Clint Adams and Meg rode into view, he realized he had chosen poorly. He moved on to his next choice, further into the Outback, away from the Junction and still a far piece from the McGregor Station.

***

"Anything?" Meg asked.

"I don't see him," Clint said, "but I can feel him. Stay on my right side, Meg."

"Are you sure he's going to fire from that side?"

"It offers more cover. I noticed on the way in that there was a copse of eucalyptus trees. That's the spot I'd pick."

"How far?"

"Still about twenty miles," he said. "If he wants to be hidden, he'll be there."

"And if he wants a high point?"

"I kinda figured where that'd be, too," Clint said.

"And what if he ain't as smart as you?"

"Then we might be in trouble."

***

The shooter reached the copse of eucalyptus trees and decided that was the place. It afforded him the best cover. He tied his horse off nice and tight, so the shots wouldn't spook him, then settled into position to wait.

***

"Okay," Clint said, reigning in. Meg stopped as well. "There are the trees."

"That's pretty far," she said.

"Not for a Martin-Henry."

"And your Winchester?"

"It's perfect."

"Clint," she said, "why don't I ride on your left?"

"That gives him a clear shot at you," Clint pointed out.

"But you said he's gonna miss with his first shot," she pointed out. "If I'm on your left, he might not even make a try."

Clint thought her suggestion over.

"You know I'm right."

"All right," he said. "I don't like hanging you out there like a target, but it makes sense."

"All right, then."

"At the first sound of a shot," he said, "you hit the dirt and stay there."

"And what will you be doing?"

"I'll be riding straight for him," Clint said. "That's likely to panic him, some."

"But the closer you get to him, the better shot he'll have," she said.

"No," he said, "the closer I get, the more he'll panic, and he'll run."

"And then what?"

"And then I'll ride him down with this fine Aussie horse your family loaned me."

"Clint," she said, "if it is Matthew, then he'll be riding an Aussie, too."

"Thanks for pointing that out, Meg."

They started forward.

***

The shooter saw that Meg was now riding on Clint's left. That would give him a better chance, for sure. He sighted down the barrel of the Martin-Henry and prepared to take his shot . . .

***

At the sound of the shot Clint turned his head, sure enough, his ear told him where it had come from. He heard the shot strike leather, which was how he knew it hadn't hit Meg, but her saddle.

As he had instructed, Meg threw herself from the saddle to the ground.

Clint jerked his reins to the left and started riding straight for that copse of trees. Two more shots came in quick succession, but he knew there was panic behind them and they went wide. After that, as he closed on those trees, there were no more shots.

The shooter was running.

***

Clint Adams was crazy.

He was riding straight into the barrel of the Martin-Henry. The shooter hastily fired two more shots and missed. After that he turned with the rifle still in his hands and ran for his horse.

Chapter Forty-Four

When Clint reached the copse of trees, he quickly saw the ground where the shooter had planted himself. This time, in his haste to run, he left all four of his spent shells. Clint didn't stop to pick them up. He rode on until he found the tracks left by the shooter's mount. He had left the copse of trees and started across the Outback flats. Clint, certain that Meg had not been hit by a bullet, took off to follow the shooter's tracks.

He rode his horse hard and fast and, before long, saw the shooter up ahead, also riding hard. Clint knew this chase would take some time, but he was determined to run the man down. Perhaps the culprit might also lead him right back to McGregor Station.

Clint rode after the man for a good hour, before he realized he wasn't heading for McGregor Station. He was heading for one of the neighboring stations, but it was still a long way off, and the horses, although bred for stamina, were winded. Clint was closing the gap, and decided to employ the Winchester 73 he had just bought.

He reined his horse in, shouldered the Winchester, and although he hated to do it, shot the horse out from beneath the fleeing man.

The animal went down, the rider flew over the horse's head and landed hard. Clint got his horse moving again, and quickly rode upon the fallen man, who was just getting to his feet.

He expected to find Matthew McGregor, but was quite surprised to find himself looking at Ben Wheeler. The man was clad in trail clothes that were now dirty and torn, and his hat was lying in the sand.

"Ben?"

Wheeler got to his feet and glared up at Clint, brushing himself off. Clint had never seen this expression on Wheeler's face before. It was one of pure hatred.

"Goddamn you, Adams," he cursed. "You're a crazy man."

"What the hell were you trying to do?" Clint demanded.

"Isn't that obvious?"

"But if you wanted to kill Meg, why not try on the ship?"

"I didn't want to do it on the ship," Wheeler said, dusting himself off. "It was only when I got to Sydney and met with Carstairs that it became necessary."

"Necessary, why?"

"To get McGregor's Station from her, of course," Wheeler said. "Carstairs was sure he could buy it from her, but when that didn't happen plans changed."

"To murder?"

"It seemed the only way," Wheeler said. "With Meg gone, Carstairs was sure he could buy the place from Matthew."

"Why would Matthew sell?"

"He wants to get out from under his family, and that place."

"Ben," Clint asked, "did you shoot at us yesterday?"

"I was one of two men," Wheeler said. "I was shocked when we both missed."

"Who was the other man?"

"I'm not going to tell you that, Clint," Wheeler said. "He and Carstairs are still going to get that place."

"Why?" Clint asked. "What's so special about it?"

"I'm not telling you that, either."

"It must be something special for the three of you to be working together," Clint said.

"I tried to buy it from Frank, but he wouldn't sell," Wheeler said. "Carstairs made a larger offer, but still the old man wouldn't sell."

"But Matthew would sell," Clint went on for him, "only he didn't inherit the place, Meg did."

"So Carstairs arranged to get her over here," Wheeler said. "I went to America so I could be on the ship and work on her, only to find you there, with her."

"Why not try to kill me on the ship?" Clint asked.

"I knew your reputation," Wheeler said. "I'm no gunman."

"Why did you recommend Kingman to Meg?" Clint asked.

"You asked me to recommend someone," Wheeler said. "It would have been suspicious if I didn't, so I recommended him."

"You weren't concerned that he might actually be helpful?" Clint asked.

"It doesn't matter," Wheeler said. "He's dead, by now."

"Carstairs had him killed, too?" Clint asked.

"Carstairs will kill the whole family if they don't sell," Wheeler said.

"The property is that valuable?"

"You have no idea," Wheeler said, but would say no more.

"All right, then," Clint said. "Let's go."

"Where? My horse is dead."

"You're walking."

"To where?"

"The Junction," Clint said. "I'm going to telegraph some law and turn you over."

"I have a reputation, Clint," Wheeler said. "It's your word against mine."

"We'll see," Clint said.

"But . . . it'll take forever to get back there."

"You're in good shape, Ben," Clint said, "and we're going to stop and pick up Meg."

"You're going to tell her it was me who was trying to kill her?"

"I sure am."

"That's too bad," Wheeler said. "You know, I was sure I could romance her on the ship, if you weren't there."

"Don't bet on it," Clint said. "She's a smart woman and would've seen right through you." He pointed the Winchester right at the man. "Hand me that Martin-Henry, and start walking."

Wheeler looked down at the fallen weapon.

"That's a good rifle."

"Hopkins bought it for you?"

"He did," Wheeler said, "under Carstairs' orders."

"That lawyer's been directing everybody," Clint said. "What made you think he wouldn't kill you, too, in the end?"

"He's killing people who were in his way," Wheeler said, "not his partners."

"You're a fool if you believe that. Come on, hand it over. It's too nice a weapon to leave here in the sand."

"It is that."

"Easy," Clint said, "pick it up with your finger through the trigger guard."

Clint truly thought Wheeler had given up, he never expected the man to straighten quickly, trying to bring the rifle to bear.

He pulled the trigger of the Winchester once, and Wheeler fell. The man had left him no choice.

"Fool!" Clint said.

Chapter Forty-Five

"You left him out there?" Meg asked.

"I wasn't about to put him over my horse and walk. I wanted to get back here and check on you."

When he had arrived at where he'd left Meg, she was sitting in the sand, waiting for him.

She stood up and listened to his story.

"Ben wheeler," she said, when he finished. "Who would've thought it? Well, I guess that clears Matthew."

"Not quite."

"Why not?"

"Wheeler said there were two shooters yesterday," Clint said.

"You still think it was Matthew?"

"James and Daniel told me Matthew rode out after we did," Clint said. "It sounds to me like he gave them a phony excuse."

"So what are you going to do now?"

"I was going to go back to the Junction and see if we could send a telegram to get some law out here," Clint said. "I wanted to turn Wheeler over to them. But now . . . I think we'll just go back and talk to Matthew. Is your horse okay?"

"He's fine. The bullet hit the saddle. Are you going to accuse Matthew," she asked. "What if he denies it?"

"I'm going to try to bluff him," Clint said, holding the Martin-Henry up, "with this."

***

When Clint and Meg walked into the McGregor house they were just about to sit down for supper, but the food was not yet on the table.

"You're just in time," Katy said.

"Any luck?" Matthew asked.

"Some," Clint said, and threw the Martin-Henry down on the table. James and Daniel jumped from their seats, but Matthew remained seated.

"What the hell—" Daniel snapped, as he and James stared down at the rifle.

"What's this?" Matthew asked.

"That's your partner's gun," Clint said.

"What're you talking about, my partner?"

"Ben Wheeler," Clint said. "He's dead, but before I killed him he gave you up."

Matthew looked at Meg.

"You believe this?"

"Every word."

"What are they talking about, Matthew?" Katy asked.

"Yeah," James said, "what's going on?"

Matthew looked at everyone staring at him, and then shrugged.

"Daddy should've left this place to me," Matthew said. "I would've sold it to Carstairs and we all would've had money."

"What?" Katy asked. "Sell our home?"

"We've got no more cattle, no more sheep, and a few horses," Matthew said. "Meg isn't going to turn things around, here. Selling's the only way."

"You can't sell, Matthew," Daniel said.

"No, you can't," James agreed. "We wouldn't go along with that."

"You'll go along with anything I tell you to," Matthew said.

"No," Daniel said, "not this. And not with trying to kill Meg."

"She's family," James said.

"She ain't no kin to us!" Matthew snapped.

"She is too!" Katy cried out. "Matthew, how could you do this?"

"I was doing it for all of us," Matthew said.

"B-but . . . not murder!" Katy said.

"Matthew," Clint said, "why do you think Carstairs wants this place?"

"I don't care," Matthew said. "He offered me a good price."

"And why do you think Ben Wheeler got involved?" Clint went on.

"What are you trying to say?" Matthew asked.

"What's on this property that you don't know about?" Clint asked.

Matthew stared at Clint and finally got it.

"Damn!" he swore.

Chapter Forty-Six

It was two days later when Clint walked into Alan Carstairs office. He did the same thing he had done at the McGregor house, he slammed the Martin-Henry down on the man's desk. Carstairs leaped out of his chair and stared.

"What the hell—what do you think you're doing, Adams?"

"Well," Clint said, "initially, I was going to kill you—but I changed my mind."

Carstairs' eyes widened.

"What are you doing here?"

"It's all over, Carstairs," Clint said. "Ben Wheeler's dead, but before I killed him he gave up Matthew McGregor, and you."

"I don't know what—"

"Also, Edward Hopkins has talked to the police, who are on their way here. He's not willing to take the fall for you. You should've picked your partners more careful-ly."

Suddenly, Carstairs relaxed.

"They thought they were partners?" he asked. "I have no partners, Mr. Adams, but you and I could change that."

"Why would I partner with you?"

"It's simple," Carstairs said. "Silver."

That surprised Clint.

"There's silver on the McGregor property?"

"Indeed," he said. "When Frank McGregor first came to me about selling, I had the property assayed. It's rich in silver in one of the mountains."

"And Frank wanted to sell?"

"Well, I made the mistake of telling him about it. He wouldn't sell after that, but he didn't have the money to mine the silver. And, apparently, he didn't tell his family about it."

"Why did he leave the property to Meg?"

Carstairs sat at his desk.

"He didn't. I falsified the will after he died. I wanted her to come here so I could buy the property from her and still keep those boys in the dark."

"And now you're making me an offer."

"That's right," Carstairs said. "A partnership. You get that lady to sell me the property, and we'll split it."

"I don't think she'll do that, Carstairs."

"Why not?"

"Because she's in the next room, right outside that door, listening to everything you say."

"What?"

"Meg?" Clint called. "Come on in."

When Meg came through the door she wasn't alone. There were two men in uniforms with her.

"Officers," she said, "I want that man arrested."

***

The charges against Carstairs were numerous, including murder. Hopkins made a deal to testify. Matthew didn't know anything, since he had been dealing with Ben Wheeler. He was in the dark about the silver.

Meg and Katy accompanied Clint to the docks to see him off. He was taking a different ocean liner home.

"Where are Daniel and James?" he asked.

"They're home, keeping an eye on Matthew," Meg said.

"Meg," Clint said, "he tried to kill you."

"He's very ashamed about that, Clint," Meg assured him. "And he's family."

"Well," Clint said, "it's up to you how you want to handle it."

"Meg is being very forgivin'," Katy said. "She's given us all even shares of the property."

"How are you going to mine that silver?" Clint asked.

"I'm talking with a bank about a loan," Meg said. "We'll get it out."

"Well then," Clint said, "I wish you luck."

Meg put her arms around his neck and kissed him soundly.

"Thank you for everything."

Katy gave him a quick hug.

He tucked his bedroll under his arm and went up the gangplank. When he was aboard, he turned and waved. He hoped he could make the trip home without hearing anything about silver, or pirates.